AngelFall

Book II

A Novel of Hell

By S.E. Foulk

AngelFall Book II

This is a work of fiction. All of the characters, organizations, and events portrayed in this novel are either products of the authors imagination or are used fictitiously.

AngelFall Book II - A Novel of Hell. Copyright © 2011 by Scott E. Foulk. All rights reserved. No part of this book may be used or reproduced in any matter whatsoever without written permission except in the case of brief quotations embodied in critical articles or reviews.
For more information send an email to: mortuus.angelfall@gmail.com
 or visit http://TheAngelFallSeries.com

Cover Art: *The Last Judgment*, by Fra Angelica, Florence, Italy 1431

ISBN-13: 978-1463690649
ISBN-10: 1463690649

First Edition: August 2011

This book is dedicated to

My grandfather, George Snow, who read to me and encouraged my inner storyteller,

and to my wife Mamo, for her love and support throughout, and the depth of character I would have not found, in myself or the beasts and beings of Hell.

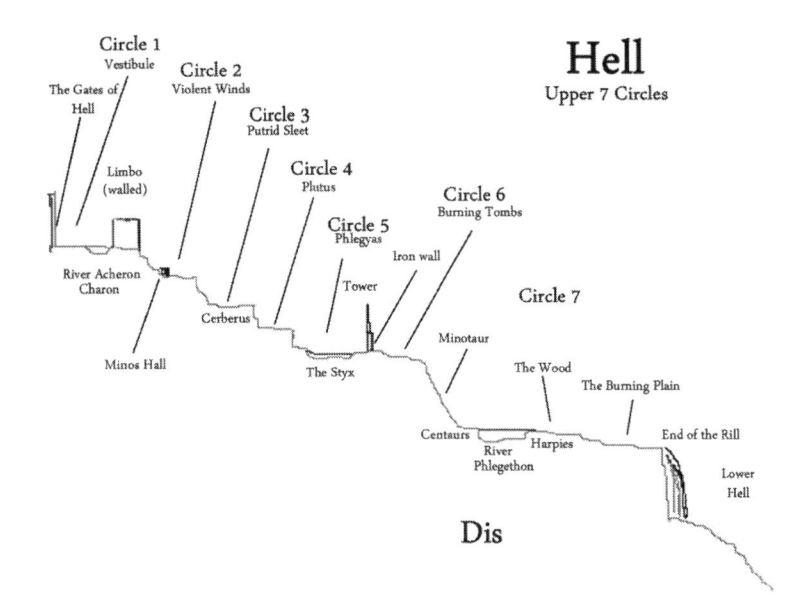

AngelFall Book II

Hell
Upper 7 Circles

- Circle 1 — Vestibule
- The Gates of Hell
- Circle 2 — Violent Winds
- Circle 3 — Putrid Sleet
- Limbo (walled)
- Circle 4 — Plutus
- Circle 6 — Burning Tombs
- Circle 5 — Phlegyas
- Iron wall
- River Acheron Charon
- Tower
- Circle 7
- Minos Hall
- Cerberus
- The Styx
- Minotaur
- The Wood
- The Burning Plain
- Centaurs
- Harpies
- End of the Rill
- River Phlegethon
- Lower Hell

Dis

AngelFall Book II

Prelude
Beginning Hell

I don't know how long I stood there. I had cried so much I couldn't cry anymore. My eyes were burning terribly, nearly swelling shut. I knew that I had to face the inevitable and I didn't want to. Ghastly sounds were constantly filling the background. It was like being outside a stadium for a big game, only, instead of cheering it was the opposite. Added to that was the horrific smell. There is no smell on earth comparable to the stench of Hell.

I wanted to tell myself that I was mistaken, that I was only in some sort of purgatory and I wondered, what happened to the part about the white light; about seeing all my relatives and the angels? I mean, I was not Good in life, but I was definitely not Bad either. Questions flowed from me along the lines of "Why me?" and "What did I do to deserve this?" I suppose this is common for everyone upon first arriving in Hell. It makes perfect sense, really.

I started walking, realizing I was tightly wrapped in some pure white, cottony material. Except for my head and neck, I was dressed like a mummy. I couldn't imagine I would have been buried in this outfit, but the cloth was comfortable enough and at this point, comfortable enough was okay by me. I was also barefoot, standing on a gravelly path leading towards a river. The path was pretty well-worn and distinguishable from the sandy muck that surrounded it. For the most part, the path was the driest area of wherever I was. I had not yet recognized that I was in Dante's Hell, because although the atmosphere was dark and dreary, it was more akin to a stormy day in Seattle rather than the pitch black of night.

A mist, lower than a cloud, floated high over my head. It was thick too, like a textured fog and it moved and swirled, never floating to the ground. I looked down the path, which veered to the left from where I arrived and I couldn't detect another soul anywhere.

On either side of the path were rolling hills, with mounds bigger in circumference than golf greens, scattered randomly and all composed of wet mucky sand. There was no visibility past those hills, not unless I went off-path and walked onto one of them. A person who thinks outside the box might have wandered off and at least taken a look. I certainly had the time and I wasn't in any particular rush to get to Hell, but I didn't venture or veer. I merely stumbled on, eventually coming to a rotted dock at the end of the path. It was on the river I had seen earlier as I approached. Had I not glimpsed the river earlier, I might have mistaken it at the dock for a lake because I couldn't see across it to the far side. Unlike rivers, the water did not flow in any direction. No swirl or eddy gave away the fact that this was a river at all. The mist floated on its surface, hiding the other shore and unlike rivers, this body of water appeared to be nothing more than a giant mud puddle that stunk of stagnation.

I stood by the dock for a few seconds when out of the murk came a shadow of a figure looming tall and large. Terror gripped my insides because if I were correct, a grotesquely foul and filthy old man, his eyes on fire, would be pulling his skiff up to the dock shortly. I wanted to be wrong; I hoped for it, but the sound of an oar striking water began to slowly fill my ears with the dread of unwelcomed truth.

Without warning, from behind me, a man sobbed out loud. I almost jumped out of my skin as I hadn't heard or seen him coming. He continued to sob even as I stood staring at him; as if he were alone and I was invisible. Which is as it should've been since I was too numb to spare any feelings of sympathy for him. I was simply too overcome with my own situation to care. And, there was no time for extraneous feelings anyway as just then, as I had been dreading, Charon's boat unmistakably emerged, pale in the mist.

The ferryman's fiery eyes were locked on us and glaring, as if we two were the reason that Hell existed. I became acutely weak with fear and froze in place. I recalled my lifetime phobia of heights; its consuming and inescapable control over me and noted this was the same feeling. The greasy obscenity jumped from his boat, yelling at us to get in as he swung a giant oar around. We moved, the two of us trying to get the furthest away from the end of the skiff where Charon had stood. I sat at the front, just behind the newer arrival, who had managed to get in faster. Charon jumped into the skiff and with a single pull we were navigated far from shore. I did not look back, for to do so would have meant having to face that horrific apparition.

The dock and the landscape disappeared as we headed into the gloomy pother. The skiff slid across the river diagonally to the left from the dock, splitting the water surface like a speed boat as Charon paddled to the far shore. We were a few minutes on the river when we cleared the mist and glimpsed stone walls lining the shore at the far side of the river. This was strange to see. I had no recollection of walls in Dante's story, yet here they were, and they had to be nearly 100 feet high. I couldn't see where we were going to land or how we would enter the next circle, there was no apparent opening.

As I studied the wall, searching for a possible landing, the newcomer began to sob again, unable to stop himself. Charon howled a second before all went red. I saw a bright flash against my eyelids - the kind you get in a fist fight when punched in the eye, except this was far worse. The flash disappeared as the pain possessed me. My left ear and my head were throbbing in a tortured agony I had never before experienced. Charon had smacked me squarely in the side of my head with his big oar, out of anger for the sobbing man.

My skull should have been crushed and I should have been killed by that deadly blow. I should not have felt the aftermath. But of course, I was already dead, so the pain continued large and long. I could do nothing except move to get out of the way of the next strike. I pulled the sobbing man toward Charon, throwing him on the boat bottom, and sat in his spot, holding my head and keeping an eye on the ferryman the whole rest of the trip. The sobbing fool was also struck by Charon's oar, but still I cursed him for causing me to be punished for his wailing. Charon's blow seemed to be enough to silence the man's weeping.

Thankfully, no more incidents occurred during the trip. I held my hand against my throbbing ear until we reached the shore. As the boat slid into the bank I jumped out, eager to create distance between myself and Charon's oar. The sobbing man did not share my eagerness, or at least my speed. I heard his screams come up from behind me as Charon's yelling became a roar. I could hear the oar connect to the sobbing man and I covered my ear again, instinctively, heading quickly down a path between two enormously high stone walls.

I must have walked down the narrow path about a mile before I saw any change in the composition of the walls. On the left, a gate appeared. It was the height of the wall, though I could not get far back enough to see clear to the top. It was cast iron, and looked impractically heavy. I don't know how it opened; no handholds were present and it was a straight flat gate, all the way up. I thought to knock, but second guessed myself. Coming up behind me was the sobbing man, bruised and limping along slowly. Strangely, in my life, I could feel sorry even for guys I was fighting with, but for this man, and in this place, my compassion was not present. I stopped examining the large gate and moved away from him.

In just a few minutes I came upon a long, curving line of what I assumed were the recently dead that I could not see the end of. The line hugged the right wall which curved around slightly as the path gradually sloped downward. The people in front of me were dressed similar to me. Some were crying and some cursed while others said nothing. I saw no one making conversation or small talk with those around them. This was the path to our final judgment and everyone was focused on their imminent sentence to damnation.

It was a terrible, grim fate, and I had to wait in line for it.

AngelFall Book II

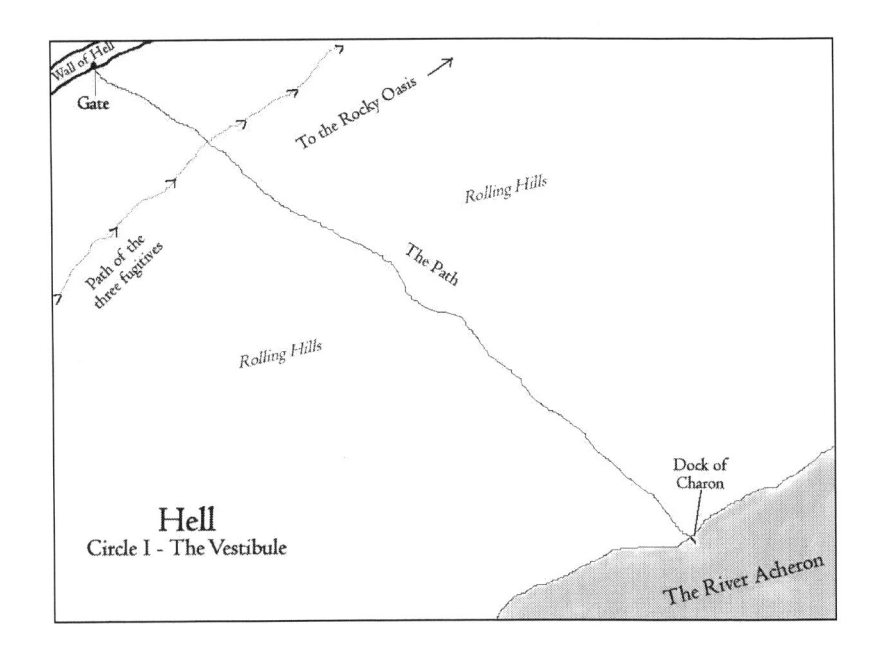

Chapter 27
The Two Fugitives

Darius sat silent, peering out from behind the boulders. He remained in hiding for a long time after his companions had been taken by the flying demons to what was assuredly a far worse fate than the torment they had previously escaped. Although no more imps or demons had visited the rocky oasis, the wait had provided too much time for Darius to anguish over his probable fate. When he emerged from hiding, Panos' and Aetos' gore lay before him, floating thickly across the pool and muddling in grotesque clumps on the stream drifting towards Acheron. Darius shuddered, trying not to imagine what lay before him.

Leaving this rocky oasis would be dangerous, but staying would insure the creatures' return. The fugitive wished he would go insane. At least that way, without the ability to rationalize, his horror might be diminished. Darius wondered if someone else would come along, another fugitive from this circle looking to escape Hell.

He had completely healed up from his wounds and regenerated back into the gaunt frame of the body with which he entered Hell. He was free of the Hell fly bites that had nearly blinded him in the Vestibule, but only somewhat free of the Vestibule's filth and dirt. Regardless of his having washed, Darius wasn't able to scrub himself free, yet Darius was content to be for the moment, safe and relatively healthy.

At long last, Darius gathered the courage to depart the rocky oasis. He planned to circle the perimeter of the boulder and stone outcropping, keeping an eye out for any approaching creatures or other fugitives. He would keep his wits sharp as he took the path from the gate to Acheron where the newcomers walked down to cross the river. No one would bother him there and he could enjoy the change in scenery, slight as it was.

Darius performed his perimeter check, and after many checks in every direction, he left the stony refuge, heading toward the path. The wall was a long distance away on his right side this time. He made it from the boulders to the path in a much shorter time than it had seemed when he and his friends were making their way to the boulders.

Darius paralleled the pathway, never stepping closer than a few meters. He watched the newly dead walk down the slightly sloping trail to the river. There were faces of myriad shapes and features but they all shared a single commonality: in their entirety, the faces expressed stories of guilt. There was the nuance of rage, victimization, and horrified shock; but as a whole, the stories were a countenance of guilt.

One man rushed over to Darius, pleading his innocence, and insisting there had been a dreadful mistake. But of course, Darius was unable to do anything about it. Darius looked at him, dumbstruck by the man's impotent denial, and his silence sent the man into a spasm of hateful cursing. After that, Darius moved further away from the path – close enough to continue observing but far enough away to discourage any more interaction.

When he reached the gate, Darius walked up to it, trying to negotiate a closer look at the opening. Perhaps there was some trick to it, some way to escape. Darius had heard of ghosts when he was alive, but he could not fathom how any avoided or circumvented Hell and visited the living. He wondered where he might go if he succeeded in stealing away. He did not relish the idea of hanging in the ether as a specter, doomed to wander the Earth as a frightening, unwelcomed stray; but better that than the eternal scourge of this nether world. Was there any way to get through the gate?

Darius checked from every angle available on his side of the wall. No luck. He walked toward the gate from each edge of the wall and from the path, over and over again. He tried to look through the doorway, but only once saw any glimmer of light. That was when a new soul had passed through. The soul, startled at first when he nearly bumped into Darius; gaped at him; taking in Darius' hardened face, his smell, his garb, his dark, haunted eyes; and then stumbled backwards in desperation, finally comprehending the gravity of his own plight. It was a dreadful moment for Darius, bringing back the grief and feelings of hopelessness he endured when he first arrived in Hell.

Darius left the gate when he was satisfied he had done all he could. Once again, his thin body paralleled the well worn trail back toward the river. Dwelling on his encounter with the newcomer, he felt lost and more alone than ever. He missed his friends greatly. Darius' head hung low, his weary eyes fixed onto the ground as he walked. Thus, Darius the fugitive was not ready for the next surprise.

Coming up the path approaching him, was a large, imposing figure of a man. Not certain why anyone would be walking away from the dock on the Acheron, in the direction of the gate, Darius leapt out of sight, scurrying towards the oasis. He was not going to wait for even a second to find out if the figure was a fugitive or a fugitive hunter. Darius ran for as much time as it took him to feel safe enough to notice he wasn't being pursued.

To his great relief, when he turned around for a quick glimpse, Darius saw that the stranger had not altered his course but was still headed towards the gate; oblivious to the presence of Darius. Darius watched the stranger with no small amount of curiosity, certain the man was mistakenly hoping to exit the gate whose mysteries had only just confounded Darius' every effort to unravel it.

Darius took in the sight of this larger than life presence; his strange, filthy apparel, his bruised and battered body and his purposeful but wounded gait. The man appeared young; perhaps he was no more than thirty years. He was more than two heads taller than Darius, with broad, strong shoulders which his dirty blonde hair rested upon. It was clear that this man had suffered a great deal of violence yet something in his demeanor suggested gentleness. This awakened a sympathetic response in Darius and he hastily retraced his steps, following the man until within speaking distance. Mindful to keep adequate space between them should he have to run, Darius was unable to keep his presence concealed. The stranger slowed, then stopped and turned around to stare at Darius.

Darius returned his gaze, examining the stranger's robes and especially his face. The man's eyes were bloodshot and swollen, carrying a weight of great sadness that seemed ancient and infinite. The pained, wraithlike expression of this man aroused no sense of danger in Darius but rather a great welling of compassion, and thus emboldened, Darius was moved to speak.

"Hail thee, stranger."

The man continued to stare at Darius.

"I am Darius." Darius nervously ran his fingers through his matted, reddish-brown hair.

Still the man made no change in expression. Darius continued.

"I have seen many come down this path from the gate, but you alone go toward it. By your garb, I see you have known much suffering and conflict, and so also, have I, in serving my sentence. If I do not offend you, please give me your name. I have been alone for a long time and I would at least share my story with you."

Still the man gave no outward expression of interest in Darius. But Darius would not yield and he pressed the gentle giant.

AngelFall Book II

"As I have stated, I am Darius." Darius waited a few moments, readying to speak again. To his delight, he was cut off.

"I am Mortuus." replied the stranger.

Chapter 28
Chiron's' Decision

"Pholus, now that you are mostly regenerated, I would like to speak to you about an urgent matter, a matter which took place when you were kidnapped by the flying beasts," said Chiron. Pholus considered Chiron's words, glad to be in the presence of his friend after having been inordinately and unusually punished by the cruel Harpies of The Wood. His insides had been ripped out by the avians, requiring most of Chiron's vital water supply to heal. Over time he would have healed by himself, but the waters of Limbo sped up the regeneration tenfold with each vial. Chiron was adamant that Pholus regain his strength, and Pholus believed he understood why. Now that he was intact, Pholus would have his suspicions confirmed.

"Pholus, I am going to Limbo." said Chiron. Chiron waited a moment, watching Pholus' face for any change in expression, expecting his surprise. Pholus merely moved his great bushy eyebrows and nodded his head in agreement. Now Chiron had the look of surprise that he had expected from his friend.

"Why do you nod in agreement?" exclaimed Chiron. Pholus smiled. He loved his friend, and he enjoyed knowing something that Chiron did not for just once. Chiron was the smartest centaur ever known in the world, even for the short duration that centaurs existed in it. Pholus, intelligent in his own right, could not hold a candle to Chiron's gift. The Master Centaur had trained kings and demigods; he had fought great monsters; he taught medicine, music, astrology, augury, weapon making, and mathematics to the sons of the ancient Gods; and he was highly regarded by the humans. Pholus was also wise, a maker of wine, but rarely mingled with the humans. He was perhaps the fiercest of the centaurs, but he was not Chiron.

"Chiron, my good friend, I am pleased to know a thing that you do not for once." Pholus grinned his horsey-toothed grin. Chiron could not help but return the favor.

"You have been building to this a long time now. Since the demons evicted you from the forbidden area, and after your last encounter with Aristotle. Change is happening, and I think you know it." stated Pholus. Chiron dwelled on Pholus' words for a moment.

"By the way, how will you leave this circle?" inquired Pholus. "Aren't the Fallen's spells still in effect? How do you plan on getting past the boundary enchantments?"

"I do not know Pholus; I will attempt to climb in a few moments. I need you to stay here and take command for now. If your fellows find I am not present, they may opt to leave on their own. You are my second in command, and it is you they follow dearly; not just due to ranking, either. During your absence, the others were united, if only for the moment, and fought alongside each other against a common enemy." Chiron continued. "They will speak a long time of the battle for the great and beloved centaur Pholus; of their proud stance and unity. Better, you will remind them of it while I am gone. They grow bored of the eternal task. Why would they not eventually tire of it, even as simple as they are? The harpies and greyhounds did us great harm in your attack and capture, but an even greater service in providing us the common enemy, and letting us forget for the moment our eternal sentence." Chiron hesitated, his demeanor softening. "I am sorry for your suffering, but I have exhausted most of my vital waters to hasten your regeneration and my departure. Should I not make it, or if I need to battle the Minotaur trying to gain the next circle, I will require your assistance."

"I will be there, my friend. Should you reach Limbo, give Aristotle my regards. I miss his visits." said Pholus. Chiron looked at his friend. He needed to tell Pholus the sad news.

"Pholus, Aristotle is the latest to be taken to the forbidden cave. Aristotle was captured by the demons recently."

The Master Centaur saw the look of surprise he had expected earlier. Pholus was shaking his head in denial. He did not want to know or believe it. Aristotle, who had wandered Hell so often and for so long, now was being held in the forbidden area cave? Pholus always shuddered when he thought of what those dragged into the cave endured. Aristotle was his only human friend. The fiercest of centaurs was beside himself, enraged at this news, then cold and deadly and calm. He looked at Chiron, then off in the direction of the caves.

"We will free Aristotle, Chiron. He is our only human friend in this place. We can amass forces, call out the demons before they can sound their horns and summon the Fallen masters, we'll have archers from all directions pointing…"

"No Pholus; it will not work." Chiron cut him off sternly. "The Fallen masters visit the cave after approximately two hundred rounds. One of our guards will watch the cave exclusively, and that guard reports to Nessus or myself. The cave has only one human occupant currently, by the count of the demons posted outside and around the cave. Something strange is going on. Otherwise, there would be no reason for someone like Aristotle, who is merely traversing Hell illegally, to be confined at that place."

"Will you just leave Aristotle to the cave?" exclaimed Pholus, incredulous.

"Do not worry" Chiron assured him, "I will not leave our friend to that fate. I just need time…and answers. Now, will you assist me in what I ask?" Pholus nodded his ready assent and Chiron continued, "In a few moments we will leave here, you to make your reappearance among your fellows, and command them away, and I to climb up to the Sixth Circle. We will go to the rockslide area, and keep a lookout for the Minotaur. You are well enough to walk now?"

"Yes" replied Pholus, full of wonder at what his friend was up to. He knew he could not encompass the thinking and strategizing that Chiron did easily in his head, and so, as usual, went with blind faith.

* * * * * *

Chiron had attempted before to escape the Seventh Circle, along with many other centaurs, by climbing to the Sixth Circle. A few of the centaurs had actually traveled the other way, deeper down into Hell, despite warnings from their fellows, and made it as far as the plains. The falling fire dispelled their attempts to escape via this route. Centaurs feared fire too much.

Chiron had begun the first climb toward the Sixth Circle in full view of the Fallen and their demon workers, who were stationed at various points above and surrounding the Rise. The rulers of hell attended the event, almost bemused, and their sycophants waited in feverish anticipation as the centaur leader made his way up the boulder-strewn Rise. It was soon after the centaurs had appeared in the Seventh Circle of Hell and they were, after surveying the entire territory allotted them, attempting to find a way out.

The Rise was the natural and logical place for the centaurs to make their ascent to the Sixth Circle. The area did not elevate vertically like the other areas around the entire Seventh Circle. The incline sloped upwards at a sufficiently favorable angle for the horse-bodied Halflings and was laden with large boulders from an ages old landslide. The four-legged centaurs could navigate this expanse more evenly and their large hooves, stepping around the rocky terrain, could gain solid footing while using the boulders as supports.

On that infamous first climb, upon reaching a point roughly one quarter of the way up, a strange and terrible invisible force, met them, pushing the ascending centaurs out into the air, off the rocks of the slope and over the boiling river. The centaurs initially howled in rage and surprise, but began yelping and whinnying as they were dropped into the boiling river Phlegethon. Eventually, all the centaurs escaped the river, assisted by their fellows. But, feisty and arrogant, once they regenerated, off the climbing herd went for another attempt. Many centaurs had been dropped into the boiling Phlegethon more than ten times before they gave up their fool's quest.

The worker demons jeered at the Halflings for their arrogance, and a single demon slapped a nearby centaur on the hind flank, ignorant of the proud nature of the beasts. In retaliation, another centaur quickly loosed an arrow into the demon's backside, but as it screamed and screeched, its Fallen master, focusing intently upon the offending centaur, whispered incantations under its breath. The centaur spattered instantly onto the ground, in a concussion of blood and gore, leaving a twitching rack of skeleton, flesh and entrails. The remaining centaurs held their arrows.

The Fallen master had the other demons remove the arrow from the rear end of their fellow. The extraction took a large chunk of meat from the beast's buttock and it fell to the sandy turf in a frenzied shriek. When the Fallen and their worker demons finally departed into the mist, they left their injured coworker lying on the bank in the midst of its regeneration. The demon's last moments were in a surround of angry centaurs, their bows fully drawn. Its grotesque noise charged the millisecond, and then was silenced by multiple arrows through its throat. The first strike was followed by arrows to its head, chest, then legs and arms. No place on its body was devoid of arrows. The arrow fletching transfigured the beast into a feathery porcupine. The centaurs then grabbed the beast by the arrows, and heartily tossed it into the river, where it sank in the boiling abyss. The final iteration of the demon made its appearance in an explosion of red liquid bursting up from Phlegethon's depths. After which, only the arrows emerged flat against the face of the river. The demon was never seen again.

From that time forward, the centaurs did not attempt to escape. It had been thousands of years and sometime during those thousands of years, the Fallen stopped dispatching their demons to patrol the Rise.

* * * * * *

Originally, the Master Centaur had climbed up the rocky incline twice, and both times he was dropped into the boiling liquid. From this experience, Chiron knew the dangers of climbing the Rise. One of these dangers included having to watch out for the Minotaur, who often ventured down the slope looking for trouble. Aristotle told Chiron he had once or twice encountered the Minotaur, getting too close for comfort, but to the good fortune of the traveler, the half-bull beast was not especially burdened with great intelligence. The Minotaur could be easily deceived and Aristotle's strategy worked for him every time. When he encountered the Minotaur, Aristotle merely hid and threw stones in another direction, whereupon the half-bull beast would roar in a rage, and turn running like a fetch dog towards the sound; continuing until it was far away. It never seemed to tire of Aristotle's trick.

With exception of the more recent development of visitations by the Fallen to the forbidden area cave, which was located in the Seventh Circle, but far from the Rise, there was no regular presence of the

Fallen or their demons around the Rise. However, there was still the danger of the confinement spell which had successfully thrown Chiron and the other centaurs from the slopes of the Rise into the boiling river below.

Chiron knew the potency of the Fallen spells, but for how long the spells lasted, he could only guess. In order to be successful with his plan, he would have to wager that the spells had run their course and were no longer in effect. It was a gamble he was ready to make.

Chiron and Pholus ordered the centaurs in the area away from the boulder-laden grade, then the Master Centaur instructed Pholus to keep a watch near the cave, and another near the rise so that Pholus would be informed when Chiron returned or if he had been captured. Chiron scanned the rockslide, looking toward the edge of the Sixth Circle and seeing no sign of the Minotaur, nodded to Pholus. He began his journey upward, toward Limbo.

Pholus watched steadily while Chiron made his way up the incline. He was relieved to see his friend still bound to the rocky slope well past the quarter way point and when Chiron at last disappeared beyond the mist, Pholus turned away, heading in the direction of the forbidden area.

Chapter 29
Socius Rebukes the Elder

Socius was beside himself. The gate guard, Philemon, had a moment ago informed him of the Elder Bracchus refusing to allow entrance to Aristotle's fugitive. Socius was in the main meeting room of the Keep, arguing with the Elder about the matter. Some of the other Elders watched, some were busy reading, pretending to ignore Socius while fully listening.

"You have no right to send anyone away from Limbo!" said Socius. "He had a signed parchment from Aristotle! Is Aristotle's word not good any longer?" The round-faced Bracchus smiled his controlled, condescending smile.

"I was doing what any good leader would do, Socius, protecting my people and their place in eternity…"

"What do you mean by 'my people', Bracchus? Surely you don't mean the people of Limbo as they never voted for you in any election." Socius smiled, counting on correct appearances to carry the day. He had stepped far over the line of decorum and he knew he must gain control over himself if he had any chance of rescuing the stranger from outside the walls of Limbo. "What I mean to say is, you were selected by a handful of Elders to your post. You should not burden yourself with speaking for the people of Limbo."

"And you should consider your words, Socius. Like it or not, I was selected by those who were *elected* by the good people of Limbo. I hold a position of great responsibility which I intend to oversee and influence to the utmost degree." Bracchus was moving his head to the side, ever so slightly, like a fat headed cobra with his hood up. "You, and Aristotle are of no consequence in these matters, and Aristotle has no sanctioned authority to invite fugitives to and endanger the safety of Limbo!"

"He is besotted with power," thought Socius, but he held his calm appearance as he bent his face toward Bracchus. "I see Bracchus. So the 'sanctity' of your appointment had nothing to do with your political ties to the other Elders?"

"It had nothing to do with my friends, Socius." Bracchus' face widened. "The welfare of my fellow citizenry is beyond question and my experiences; I would say my nature particularly qualifies me to this post."

"Yes of course, your experiences and your nature," mumbled Socius. He had several retorts to Bracchus' arrogance, but dare he say them?

It was rumored Bracchus had been a ruthless Governor of his province during his lifetime. A citizen of Bracchus' province also had been sentenced to eternity in Limbo. When he observed the climb of Bracchus into the council of the Elders, the man went into hiding and had only been seen since on rare occasions by very few, trusted individuals. Bracchus dispatched a small regiment to find the witness, but the search was fruitless. The man's story had reached Socius' ears as well as many of the guards and citizenry of Limbo. He stated that he had been a farmer who was taxed out of his land and home by the legislation of the wealthy Governor Bracchus. He and the other afflicted landowners began meeting with the local townspeople, discussing their options against the greed of Bracchus. When Bracchus got word of their assemblages, he had them executed publicly, without a trial, for treason. There was no reason to doubt the man, he had nothing to gain from telling either the truth or a lie in this situation.

"You are a stupid boy, Socius," remarked the Elder dismissively, "I am a busy man. I will thank you not to waste my time anymore."

"Truly, I am young in appearance Bracchus. But remember, I am several centuries old and the student of one of the great minds of all time. World histories praise him still. Is it not our privilege to follow his counsel and carry out his wishes whether we understand them or not? After all, can you say you know more than Aristotle?"

"You test my patience, *boy*. We have nothing more to discuss! Your fugitive will never be allowed into Limbo. That's the end of it," Bracchus looked around the room triumphant, and was caught unaware.

"I wonder how *you* managed to get into Limbo then, Bracchus, since mass murder is such a severe crime?"

That was it. Socius' temper had got the better of him and the war of words found it's first quarry. Socius' immediate self recrimination was arrested by the enraged Elder who slapped the youth squarely in the face. "You will regret ever…"

Bracchus was stopped as abruptly when reflexively, Socius threw his palm into the abdomen of the chubby Elder. The deft maneuver of Socius launched the Elder across the room. Socius walked toward him, calmly looking down on the pained, frightened Elder. The other Elders were out of their miscellaneous poses of indifference, aroused now and calling for the guards to restrain Socius. But the guards had witnessed the entire incident and had already grabbed Socius by his arms. Ferris, the captain of the guards, approached Socius along with the Elder, Alcander.

"He has struck an Elder, Ferris. He should be thrown into the dungeon!" postured Alcander.

"The Elder struck first." said Ferris. "By your laws he should be thrown into the dungeon also."

"Bracchus is an upstanding member of …"

"We all saw Bracchus strike Socius first, Alcander," nodded Ferris to the guards who surrounded Socius. "*Upstanding* members do not strike anyone. If you prefer to have Socius thrown into the dungeon, then I will do the same for Bracchus. You decide."

Alcander stood quiet, red in the face. "Let him go then!" he yelled, "But he comes into this building no more! Help Bracchus up."

The stunned Bracchus was heavy, and it took two guards to lift him from the stone floor. He was still very much incapacitated from Socius' blow. Socius was also released.

"Bracchus, if you wish to strike me," spoke Socius in an oddly ameliorating yet defiant tone, "Come to the fields when we have our battle games. Perhaps you could show me what you've learned about the lessons of power."

"Socius. You will leave now." said Ferris, who then turned to address the guards helping Bracchus. 'Take the Elder to his chambers."

"Bracchus had no right to turn anyone away," Socius repeated as he looked Alcander in the eyes.

"Do not return here again Socius. The next time I see you in here you will be on your way to the dungeon." Alcander grit his teeth angrily, but Socius ignored Alcander, and turned to leave. He had an idea brewing and needed to enlist some help.

The guards were generally always friendly toward Socius, though not as much toward Aristotle. Socius was a favorite among many of the people of Limbo, particularly the warrior types who had trained with him and enjoyed their battle games. Nevertheless, the guards were directly under the command of the Elders, and could not blatantly or openly disobey them. That is why, however reluctant, they were more inclined to obey the command of Bracchus rather than side with Socius. In spite of this, it was the guards who had dispatched Philemon to notify Socius of the stranger's arrival and subsequent refusal of entry.

Socius headed toward Elysius, a fragrant meadow of grasses and trees that scented the air with a perfume of earthy forest. The freshness never grew old here. Many of the warriors would regenerate in Elysius after each mock battle. The warrior leaders, the General's Council, were almost always present during and after these battles, working on game plans by creating or revising strategies and discussing prior battle weak points with their men. It was Socius' favorite place to hear their old war stories, too. Socius had come here since his early childhood, a way to escape from his less interesting lessons. The teachers always knew where to find him when he was late for tutoring. His frequent clamoring for the old timers' battle stories endeared him to the ancient warriors.

Once Socius arrived at Elysius, he saw Militus, one of the generals who had tutored him in the arts of combat. Militus sat in the middle of the field, reading a scroll from the Great Library. The familiar sight brought the resolve of clarity to Socius. Militus was the very one Socius hoped to find and he considered this meeting an auspicious one. Militus always had an open ear for Socius, and if there was anyone who could enlist warriors to assist Socius in carrying out his plan, it would be Militus. Seeing the boy approach, the old warrior smiled. Socius knew at this moment he would get the aid he required.

He only hoped the Fallen would not find the fugitive stranger first.

Chapter 30
New Friends in Exile

Mortuus sat, still lingering in depression and hopelessness, but lighter now. Darius, a friendly wanderer who appeared to be well into his forty years, had approached Mortuus on his way to the gate. Darius had to follow Mortuus nearly up to the gate before he could talk Mortuus out of making the futile attempt. Initially Mortuus was angry with Darius for interrupting his mood with what he deemed frivolous talk of friendship. Mortuus' recent rejection at the gate of Limbo still hurt and he was not interested in building up empty hope with equally empty chatter.

Despite Mortuus' rebuff, Darius would not be dissuaded and finally he was allowed to lead Mortuus to the rocky outcropping. Darius had encouraged Mortuus to clean himself before deciding on his next actions. As Mortuus followed him to the oasis, Darius talked about his two friends and how they had been carried away up into the air. This account piqued Mortuus' interest as he had earlier seen some of the same sort of flying creatures, though only one victim was discernible from his vantage point. He had wondered about the fate of the unlucky fellow.

Mortuus then recounted his own story of emerging from unconsciousness, and escaping from an underground passageway. It sounded to Darius as though his new friend had been hidden, but neither could fathom why anyone would be hidden and kept unconscious in Hell. There were too many questions, for both Mortuus and Darius.

The large man had no memory of anything before being woken up, and the awakening was so painful, he was loathe to discuss it. He wanted to get into Limbo and sate his thirst with more of the vials of water that had been left to him. Mortuus told Darius what he had sensed when the gates to Limbo had opened momentarily; the fresh, clean air, and the earthy scent that was on the guards. It was decidedly different from the rest of Hell; Hell's constant wailing and moaning coming from the depths; Hell and its ever changing, stinking odor that one could not get used to. Limbo also lacked the immediate and inexorable overwhelm of Hell's hopelessness.

Mortuus, his thirst burning, drank from the spring, cautious at first, and then ravenously. The water was refreshing, though not as restorative as the vials from Aristotle. When his thirst was finally quenched, he washed in the spring as Darius nervously kept watch at the perimeter of the rocky oasis. The water was the first that Mortuus had bathed in since awakening. It was rejuvenating, although he was initially distracted and then transfixed as his eyes began tracking the filth of lower Hell riding off his body, pressing obscenely against the clean water, and slowly drifting down the stream toward Acheron.

Mortuus, his body still bleeding slightly from his encounter with Plutus, shuddered. The pool was cool and seemed to draw out his pain and anger in the same way that it washed away the filth from his skin, his face and hair. He began feeling stronger and more relaxed. While washing his robe, he noticed his hands bore the marks of bruising and of abrasion. He noticed as well that his robe was heavier and much more sturdily woven than Darius' apparel. It absorbed a great deal of the pool water and took a long time to dry even though Mortuus had wrung it out several times.

Darius' garment was merely a death shroud; Mortuus had a full robe that became clean when washed. In comparison, Darius' death shroud was permanently stained from the mud of the Vestibule, his blood and other body fluids emanating from the constant attacks of the

Hell Flies. No matter how many times Darius had washed his shroud, he could not rid it of its tormented memories.

During his cleanse, Mortuus was pensive, reflecting on his journey hoping to organize his thoughts. The cooling waters worked its magic, easing his inner chaos enough for Mortuus to think clearly until at last he knew what he had to do. His arrival at a decision, on the other hand, created another dilemma and that dilemma was Darius. What would his new traveling ally, this fellow fugitive, think of his decision? Would they part ways, and if so, how would Darius manage on his own? Mortuus could feel Darius had formed a certain attachment of fates, if you will.

"Darius, please come here."

"Yes, Mortuus," responded a curious Darius as he walked over to the pool, taking a last, quick glance skyward.

"Darius, I have decided to go back to Limbo." Mortuus examined Darius' face for signs of any change. "I will return and try to get into the gate again. I must. It is my only hope to find out who I am and why I am here. You know your identity, and your origin, and how you came to be here. I have no knowledge of mine." Mortuus turned intently to face Darius. "But what of you? Will you come along and journey out of your relative safety? I do not know if I can get into Limbo, but I was invited by the one who awakened me. He is called Aristotle."

Darius' eyes lit up in surprise. He had heard of Aristotle in his life many times – the great teacher, scientist, mathematician, and philosopher. He had died long before Darius' birth, but was legendary. Did Mortuus speak of *the* Aristotle as the one who had awakened him?

"Darius, why do you seem surprised? Is it some…"

"You say 'Aristotle', Mortuus? He woke you? And he is in Limbo, waiting for you? *The* Aristotle?" Darius could not contain his excitement.

Mortuus considered him for a moment. "Yes, I suppose. Phlegyas, the oarsman, regarded him quite highly as well. I do not know who *the* Aristotle is that you refer to, but I would guess this would be him," nodded Mortuus. "Aristotle was known by the guards of Limbo, too. They showed a bit of deference f…"

"I will journey with you." interrupted Darius, in a great rush, now quite enthusiastic. Mortuus was dumbfounded for the moment – he would have liked to have finished his statement, but he had his answer, and Darius was not angry or disappointed.

"Good." he smiled. "I would like to leave when my clothing has fully dried." Darius returned to the perimeter of the rocky oasis, scanning for trouble, and abuzz for their next adventure.

The pair of fugitives decided to follow the path to the river, starting from as close to the gate as they could get. They hoped that it would appear to Charon they had entered as all other newcomers did. Hopefully the ferryman would forget he had earlier transported Mortuus from the Limbo side of the river. If they walked along the bank to the landing, Charon would surely recognize them as fugitives, and deny them transport, and worse, inform the demon fugitive hunters of their presence in the area. It would ruin all their hopes of getting across Acheron and into Limbo.

Mortuus told Darius how Charon had denied him passage unless given something of value. He gave a good description of the small, flat metal disc that he found while crossing the Fourth Circle. The disc had an embossed picture on it and it was the only item he would part with because it was not given to him by Aristotle. Charon had eyed it in amazement, his glaring red eyes looking back and forth from the coin, (as Darius had called it), to Mortuus. Mortuus remarked that he was relieved he had picked it up before meeting Charon because Charon seemed at the time as if he would start beating Mortuus with his oar, such was his raging temperament. On the other hand, Darius' last crossing had been well over a thousand years prior, upon his death. Darius thought that his face would not be memorable to Charon, who ferried every single one of Hell's inhabitants since time immemorial.

After much walking, the two allies finally approached the landing, nervousness rattling their insides, causing great unease. Four men were waiting at the landing when they arrived; two were crying quietly, another was pulling his hair out in an angry display of rage, and the last one was cursing to himself loudly. The angry man looked around like a cornered dog, ready to strike at anyone who ventured too close. The four barely noticed the arrival of Mortuus and Darius.

The water's edge was muck, and the dock a rotting set of timbers. In the distance, on the vaporous river, they could hear the water moving in slow rhythmic strokes, though they could not see Charon or his vessel. The slowness of the strokes served to heighten the anxiety of the doomed group. Then, like a great monster appearing from the depths, the long skiff formed out of the mist, and the glowing red eyes of the old bearded one glared out, boring holes into each of the six waiting men. One of the new arrivals sobbed loudly, blurting uncontrollably as his horror was confirmed.

Darius also turned away, unable to look into the raging red eyes of the ferryman. It felt to Darius as if the ferryman could see his guilt plainly, maybe even remember taking him the first time. The Vestibule escapee thought he would change his mind and run away, back to the safety of the rocky oasis, alone forever, but safe from the first of Hell's monsters. Darius considered that he might even prefer serving his sentence; anything seemed better than facing Charon.

Mortuus, having dealt with Charon recently, was slightly less intimidated, but still found the experience frightening. He looked around to see the effect the monstrous glaring eyes had on the others. Disturbingly, Darius looked as if he was going to flee. Mortuus stared at Darius, willfully, silently trying to lock Darius's eyes away from Charon's, and stop his flight. Darius, mustering all his courage and willpower, looked away from the ferryman. He moved his eyes around, from the skiff, to the landing, then at the newcomers, who were now all crying loudly. Then Darius noticed Mortuus, staring directly at him. Mortuus had an unmistakable calming effect for Darius; he quickly regained his composure, keeping his eyes averted for the time being.

The skiff bumped the dock, and one of the weeping men was startled. Charon leapt out, his large oar in hand, and examined all the waiting men directly. His face, close up, was even more fearsome, as the wrinkles seemed to be hundreds of small scars carved into a shape that highlighted his glowing eyes. Holding his upraised oar in his right hand, he beckoned everyone to board the large skiff with his left. Darius looked away, then back at Charon. His eyes always seemed to be staring directly into Darius. Shakily, he got into the long skiff, and stepped uneasily toward the front. Mortuus was the last one to board, and stepped into the skiff carefully. He balanced himself clumsily as Charon began pulling the large oar through the water, propelling the craft and its passengers into the mist.

Without warning, Mortuus thudded flat onto his face after the large oar connected forcibly with the back of his head. The glowing-eyed ferryman was ominous as he stood over Mortuus's laid out form; the other passengers, including Darius, cringed at the front end of the boat. Mortuus was semi-conscious, blinded by the pain of the blow.

"Who are you that traverses Hell freely, fugitive?" roared Charon. "I remember every one whom I ferry, especially those that pay to go the wrong way."

Charon looked toward the front of the boat, glaring straight at Darius.

"You are no newcomer either, fugitive."

Chapter 31
Charon's Rage

The long skiff was far from the shore, the mist almost hiding the bank of the Vestibule. Mortuus lay across the bottom, his back uncomfortable and his head in throbbing pain, so much that he could not stand up. Charon stood over him and was swearing loudly. Mortuus could hardly understand him, as flashes of yellow pain were causing his closed eyes to throb. His ribs were bruised from the force of the sudden fall, and the gnarled old man-monster was raising his oar, preparing for another blow to Mortuus' skull. Mortuus lay unaware of the impending violence; his only thought, outside of the terrible pain, was that he had been captured.

"You would have been better off staying in your own circle, fugitive." said Charon. "The demons will make you wish you had." Looking down at Mortuus, whose face was vulnerable on the left side - the right side being pressed against the boat floor - Charon straddled over him to get a better angle for the next blow. The ferryman kicked Mortuus in the side with each step, almost breaking his ribs. Mortuus yelled and rolled over painfully to see the oar completely lifted up, ready for the downward swing into his skull. Before the stroke finished its descent, Darius' thin body lunged forward from the huddle of cowering men and took the full force of the blow on his left forearm. The bones snapped soundly and he screamed in pain. Charon, enraged at missing the stroke, roared at the insolence, swearing oaths at the grimacing Darius, who was clutching his broken arm and trying to push the bones back into the flesh. Darius knew this worker from Hell would surely destroy him, but decided he would not lose another ally without a fight.

Charon pulled back his oar and stepped forward toward Darius, still straddling Mortuus. He stared into Darius with angry intent. No passenger had ever taken a stance so much as mumbling angrily under their breath in Charon's presence. Charon answered that kind of dissent without prejudice; one blow with the great oar was a cure all.

* * * * * *

Impertinence occurred rarely, and was only the result of interactions with Charon's fellow workers, the demons. On one occasion, Charon had thrown two fugitive hunters, non-flyer demons, into Acheron. The beasts had appeared on the Limbo-side of the river, demanding passage to the Vestibule from Charon without payment.

They hurled threats at the ferryman, cursing him and stating he would join the tormented in a lower circle if he did not transport them. Charon brandished his great oar as he stood his ground, threatening the demons with a bloody beating and a swim in Acheron. Furious, the demons advanced, but Charon, swinging his weapon as though it were a light wooden switch, promptly repelled the beasts back on shore, nursing their swollen heads and broken ribs. When they returned later, still bloodied, they tendered a single coin each to Charon. They boarded and were ferried across to the Vestibule.

When they had to make their way back to the Limbo side of Acheron, they appeared on the landing, now swollen and in foul moods from multiple Hell fly bites. Charon again refused them passage. They displayed their coins, but still stupidly arrogant, told Charon they would pay when they arrived at the opposite shore.

Charon transported them across Acheron while considering his options. A half second after the skiff landed, the ferryman beat the demons until they could not fight back. He picked up their coins, and then threw both far out into the filthy river. The demons sank beneath the surface like rocks and disappeared into the river depths forever.

* * * * * *

The ferryman had never experienced such insolence from human passengers prior to his encounter with Darius and Mortuus. Charon swung horizontally and missed, as Darius ducked, causing Charon to stumble and become even more enraged. He caught his balance, clumsily raising the oar above his head, sure not to miss the cringing Darius with a direct downward blow. But with Charon's rage distracting his attention, Mortuus was able to curl his legs up, unnoticed, right under Charon's groin. In an instant, Mortuus swung his lower trunk up so that his knees were nearly touching his chin and, aiming the soles of his feet at Charon's undercarriage, thrust his legs upward so hard that when they met their target, his legs cramped from the excessive effort.

The push propelled the thick-bodied ferryman in a trajectory high into the air and over the back side of the boat. He lost his great oar while in the air and it fell with a thud onto the swampy water and was taken under. Charon himself was in utter shock as he roared and flailed wildly, landing ten meters from the back side of his skiff, into the river of pain. The splash from his impact on the surface was disproportionate in its displacement of the water in that Charon landed flat, barely sending up a splash, then sunk like a big stone and vanished into unknown depths. No bubbles marked his entry into Acheron's filthy wash.

He was just gone.

Mortuus sat up, his head still hurting immensely. Darius, staggering and in pain, held his right arm gingerly; smiling weakly at his new friend. They had won, for the moment. Overwhelmed by the event they had just witnessed, the new arrivals stared at Mortuus, frightened he would throw them overboard next. Huddled together in the front of the boat, they did not move.

It turned out the skiff had enough momentum to reach the shore from Charon's initial few pulls of his oar. Several minutes later it skidded onto shore, and the newcomers jumped off hastily. They followed the path down between the two walls that defined the end boundaries of Limbo, disappearing from the sight of Darius and Mortuus, who got out of the boat much slower. The two sat on the rocky path for a long time, waiting for their wounds to heal and their pain to ease. They couldn't help but continue looking toward the river, not fully convinced Charon had been lost to Acheron. At length, they began to speak.

"How is your arm, Darius?" asked Mortuus first. "It does not appear swollen any longer."

"The pain is fading, though I do not believe my arm is nearly healed enough." replied Darius. Darius was thin and timid from his years living under the poor conditions of an impoverished slave. Besides taking the chance of leaving the Vestibule, his action in Charon's boat was the bravest thing he'd ever attempted and left him shaken up inside. It also had the odd effect of creating excitement in him. Though his arm was in the process of regenerating and therefore in discomfort, Darius was surprised at how well his meager body responded to the challenge. "I might be thin," he thought, "But I am sturdy!" He lifted his head and straightened his shoulders before turning to Mortuus. "Does your head feel better?" he asked.

"It feels better than it would have if that old monster cracked it with his oar again. Thank you for your intervention." His head was throbbing, and his vision slightly blurred, but it had gotten better. His nose had been broken and bloodied in his fall against the boat bottom, but no longer was it stinging.

"That was quite a powerful kick," marveled Darius, happy to be in a conversation of the winning side of a hard-fought battle, "You actually threw Charon from his own boat! You must have been some great warrior or athlete in your lifetime."

Mortuus smiled. His head was too achy to enjoy any boasts, but he mulled over Darius's words as they returned to him the pain of his memory loss. "I wish I knew about my lifetime, Darius. I wish I knew." He was reminded as well of their mutual goal to enter Limbo and knew he had to be more forthright about Darius' chances at the gate. Mortuus continued warily, "I have been thinking that maybe you will not be able to get into Limbo, as we spoke of. What will you do if that happens? I have to go in – I have to find out who I am and why I am here. But I worry for you."

Darius reckoned with this possibility sadly. He had already known it would be a long shot, but hadn't let that probability get in the way of his decision to join Mortuus. "I will wait outside the gate for a while if this comes to be. I may search for my friends or try to return to the Vestibule. It may be quiet and lonely, but I will not suffer the torments. If you should ever venture from Limbo, look for me."

"I will be sure to," promised Mortuus.

"It is well enough. Now, I do not wish to linger in anticipation." Darius felt his legs under him and rose with some discomfort. "Shall we be off on our next adventure?" His care-free determination, meant to supplant the woe of an impossible situation. In truth, Darius could not bear to be separated from his friend and left alone once more. Mortuus, his head throbbing, nodded and got up slowly. He could see the pain in Darius's face, but they both knew there was nothing more to say.

No sooner had they resolved to move on, than the pair, still sore and aching, froze. A small company of heavily armed men were running straight at them with dangerous intensity. Within seconds, the armed squadron had their weapons pointed directly at the faces of the two. The fugitives were forced down, back into their sitting positions; staring incredulously at the array of lethal weapons aimed at them.

They were captured.

Chapter 32
Chiron's Promise

Since his imprisonment in the Seventh Circle ages ago, Chiron had not the occasion to traverse Hell; the spell confining him and all centaur-kind left no possibility for travel. Now here he was in the Sixth Circle, trotting amongst the glowing tombs and coffins, headed for the gates of Dis. He surveyed the area, examining the heat distorted landscape as he searched for worker demons and imps. He was thinking about the failure of the confining magic that was used to contain the herds in the Seventh Circle when he picked up the familiar, dangerous scent of the Minotaur.

Chiron thought the creature might have spotted him exiting the Seventh Circle. The Master Centaur sniffed the air again, sensing the presence of the beast. This was the closest he had come in thousands of years, but how could that be, he thought. Was the Minotaur not confined to the slope area, and to the burial containers of the inner edge of the Sixth Circle? Chiron was far from the area of confinement for the beast.

The Minotaur was not a discrete half-animal, but similarly to Chiron, it had been imprisoned in its part of Hell by magical enforcement. Now the Minotaur was shadowing Chiron as he made his way toward the Styx and Phlegyas. The Master Centaur detected the Minotaur coming up from the back left. The odors of Hell were ever shifting, always to a new foul version that could not be gotten used to, but just past that odor, Chiron could perceive the wafting odor of the bull Halfling, a mix of stinking sweat both bovine and human.

The Minotaur was closing in on him. Chiron stopped and looked back, surveying the area when suddenly, from behind a stack of coffins, the Minotaur sprang up, apparently having burned itself on one of the red hot coffins; indicated by the way it held its hands on its hind quarters. Its position revealed, the bull-human stood erect, staring at Chiron across the separation of two rows of red tombs. It was enormously built, completely muscular, but with the head and lower body of a great bull. It was a fearsome creature, but awe inspiring to behold. Chiron stared at its face fully for the first time and noted something in its bull's eyes. Though they glared an angry red at the Master Centaur, it seemed that the creature was sad.

The Halflings studied each other and for a moment, Chiron was moved to compassion. Un-notching the arrow from his bow (he had automatically loaded a shaft as soon as he detected the scent of the Minotaur), Chiron approached the lone creature carefully, lowering his arms and replacing his arrow to clearly display his peaceful intention. The Minotaur scrutinized each step, growling in a low tone until the Master Centaur stopped two meters away.

"I am known as Chiron. Do you have a name?" asked Chiron. The creature was mute for an uncomfortable length of time as it weighed the words of Chiron. Finally, the Minotaur broke the silence with a deep and powerful voice that matched the countenance of the half-bull; the voice was gruff and booming.

"I am...Asterion. I am feared and hated by all who know me. Never before has anyone tried to address me. Why do you speak to me thus? There is no fear in your voice. I know fear, its smell, and I would have ripped you apart had I detected it upon your person. My enemies all had much fear, and they hated me for it. Do you not hate me also, Master Chiron?"

"You are half-bull, Asterion. I am half-horse. I have never hated anyone for being half-human. You are known for many atrocities during your time in the infamous Labyrinth, the killings of the innocents sacrificed. Your brutal violence is your legacy, but who are you now as we speak?"

"I am that monster of which you tell. But hear me. I was not always thus." said Asterion. "In my youth, my mother cared for me well, and I loved her very much. She was taken from me by her husband, Minos, her greedy, stupid husband, who threw me into a pit for many years." Asterion was beginning to speak angrily. "The dolt begat my birth by betraying Poseidon, who caused my mother to go mad and seek companionship with a great white bull. Thus, was I born, then taken away, and punished for my parentage and deformity. Once a day the fool king sent a tormentor to my pit, and he would beat me, saying "A beast must be beaten because he is only a beast." This occurred from my earliest childhood memory, everyday until I came of age. One day I fought back, killing the torturer and his guards, who had before this time laughed as I cried in torment, jeering at my suffering. Hungry and undernourished my entire life, I ripped out and ate his beating heart, and I grew strong. Thus, my placement was secured, and my reputation, in the cursed maze."

Chiron listened to Asterion tell his story. It did not much diverge from the life stories of his fellow centaurs. Most had tormented childhoods, and had been pushed to hatred and rage, eventually acting out with violence, killing or abusing others. Now the Minotaur stood here, telling his own tale, and it resembled the Halfling-kind story too well. The Minotaur had been, like all centaurs, persecuted because he was half-animal. Chiron's circumstances and intelligence were different, and so his path differed greatly, but they both ended up in Hell.

At the end of Asterion's story, the Halflings stood more comfortably in each other's presence. Chiron's compassion had been stirred; he spoke to Asterion in a more caring voice, instead of his usual commanding tone. The Minotaur was actually a very emotionally sensitive creature. Chiron could not fathom how Asterion had endured his life of extreme abuse to reach adulthood. The pair continued talking for a length of time before Chiron finally forced the conclusion of their meeting.

"Asterion, I am on my way toward the First Circle. I must leave you for now. If you wander this place, outside of your confinement area, you may be spotted and stopped, and maybe tormented like the humans. I would meet with you upon my return, and perhaps you will come and visit my circle, meet with my centaur kindred, and end your lonely patrol. For now, I must go. I have very important business needing my attention. I do not mean to abandon you, and I will make good on my promise that you join us. But please, return to your appointed patrol grounds for just a short while longer. And do not enter the Seventh Circle without my presence. The centaur regiments will not allow your visit, and I would prefer to see you unharmed."

The Minotaur was saddened, but looked into the intelligent Master Centaur's unflinching eyes. Asterion turned away, leaving Chiron. He headed toward the rocky slope and disappeared into the heat distorted Sixth Circle.

Chiron continued his movement toward the outer wall of Dis. He could finally see the wall. It was a dirty, dark, rust-stained metal, with a greenish mold growing on it. Here and there the buildings attached to the wall revealed doorways and steps to the turrets, or interiors that were on the top of the wall. In the distance, on his right, Chiron could see a flame, bursting in the air, barely visible through the mist. He saw many of the small creatures, which he recognized as imps; they cowered away upon seeing him.

* * * * * *

Long ago, the imps used to wander down on a regular basis to the Seventh Circle. The flyers, those imps with functional wings, would attack the humans who frequented the shallower portions of Phlegethon. It didn't take long before would-be victims of the little beasts learned to pull them down into the river, causing them to shriek and screech as the centaur patrols laughed loudly. Other imps attacked the centaurs, biting their shoulders as they flew from above while their ground-bound, non-flyer coworkers attacked the legs and hooves. Why the smallish creatures would attack the much larger, faster centaurs was a mystery. The packs of vermin were soon exterminated by the centaurs, who considered it great sport to 'smoke' the beasts with a single arrow. In subsequent encounters, the centaurs made it their policy to shoot on sight and the imps eventually figured out they were not a match for the much larger, stronger, skilled warriors. They did not visit the Circle of Phlegethon again.

* * * * * *

Chiron arrived at the gate of Dis, and was surprised by its large size, but then spied the small side door. It was a tight fit for his Halfling frame, but he pushed through. On the way in, Chiron saw the swamp that was the Styx, and the full size of the tower, from base to peak. It was a misty place; noises came from out of the vapors, screams and splashes of the human inhabitants, inflicting violence upon each other. Nearer to the landing, small trails of bubbles denoted the submerged existence of the tormented.

Chiron waited on the landing. He knew not to get near the swamp edge, at least not until Phlegyas arrived. He knew this from the stories of Aristotle. The oarsman would be very surprised to see the Master Centaur, and Chiron was concerned that Phlegyas might not be willing to transport him across the Styx. Chiron had no vials to exchange for his passage. He had used the last of the healing waters on regenerating Pholus from the harpy wounds. A steady, rhythmic paddling sound indicated that Phlegyas was approaching. Chiron would soon find out if the oarsman would carry him over the Styx.

To his great relief, Phlegyas was overjoyed. The two had much to talk about, each quickly recounting their past attempts to abandon their posts, and each had incurred the usual consequences. Phlegyas had spent time in the swamp when he had tried to climb up the wall to the Fourth Circle. He had reached the halfway point when he was thrown far into the Styx, like the centaurs, who had been cast into the

Phlegethon. Unlike the centaurs, he had been detained by the vicious inhabitants, and it took years to crawl out of the swamp. When Phlegyas emerged, he swore never to attempt escape again. Ever since, he remained the oarsman of the Styx.

Suddenly Phlegyas, reminded of the urgency and danger surrounding their encounter, motioned Chiron to get into the skiff, warning him not to get near the sides or the tormented of the swamp would pull him in. "We should get you out of sight, my friend, into the middle of this swamp, concealed within the mist. If the demons see you, they will attack, and worse, notify the Fallen." Phlegyas turned the boat outward, and pushed off the shore. Hidden by the mist, they continued their exchange of news and information and by the end of the journey across the Styx, had made plans to reunite again. Chiron explained to Phlegyas why he had undertaken the treacherous trip; their mutual friend had been taken into the forbidden area cave. Phlegyas was angered at this, but not so surprised.

"Aristotle was always taking chances by traveling through Hell." he said. "I told him on many occasions that it was only a matter of time before he got caught. I believe you also foresaw this happening - according to Aristotle?"

"Yes. I did, though it took no power of augury to divine his capture." said Chiron. "But why do they hide him? Hell is not secretive about torture, and there are many places Aristotle would find inescapable. What reasoning is behind this?"

"I have some information." replied Phlegyas. "Recently, I transported someone who Aristotle had awoken, a strange, large prisoner from another secretive torment."

"Awoken?" replied Chiron. "What do you mean, 'awoken'? Who sleeps in this place?"

"I mean it the way it sounds" said Phlegyas. "I do not know where the stranger was kept, except that it was a secret underground area of the burning tombs. Aristotle called it the Undertomb, and he told me only that the awakened prisoner would need transport if he made it to the swamp landing. The prisoner made it, much to my surprise and I transported him across, but while doing so, I learned that he had no memory of his past." Phlegyas stopped for a moment, looking at Chiron steadily, "Strange things are happening, my friend, many strange things; like your escape, Aristotle's capture – by the way, why do you journey to Limbo? Are you aware they may report you? I have spoken with Aristotle about the governance. They have become very bureaucratic. When I last spoke to Aristotle, I got the impression– "

"Wait, please." snapped Chiron. His inner eye had flashed - he quieted Phlegyas with a wave of his hands.

* * * * * *

Chiron was standing in a large room with older, well-dressed humans when a young man of roughly nineteen years of age entered the room. One of the elder humans stood up, looking at the boy, motioning him to remain silent as he gestured to another human to close the door. The man pulled the doors shut. The elder man addressed the young man.

"Well, Crucio?" asked the standing human expectantly.

"Yes, Elder." said the young man. "They have apprehended Aristotle behind the Hall of Minos. Demons flew off with him toward the depths."

"Then it is done." said the Elder. "You have served your people well, young man. You have the thanks of your leaders." The Elder smiled, approving of this young man's deeds. Chiron watched the boy leave.

* * * * * *

He was back, standing with Phlegyas again in his boat. He apologized heartily, and informed the oarsman of what he had just experienced.

"This has to do with Aristotle's capture." said Chiron. "The youth said he saw Aristotle taken – this has already transpired. I have recently had another vision, in which I participated, but it was somewhere else, a lake of filthy ice. A battle was imminent between the centaurs and the Fallen. By the dead! The past is always easier to see than the future." Chiron trailed off. "I must hasten my ascent to Limbo, Phlegyas."

"My friend, you will have to be very careful in Limbo – I imagine you will cause a great stir. Those Elders betrayed Aristotle to the Fallen. They are probably watching his young charge, Socius. You may want to warn him."

"I intend to." said Chiron. The Master Centaur stepped out of the boat which had grounded into the gravely shore while he was having his vision. "I will see you again Phlegyas; it has been good meeting you. You have my thanks for your transport services."

Phlegyas watched his friend gallop away, heading for the point in the wall where he could climb up to the Fourth Circle. He then realized he had forgotten to tell his friend something, of utmost importance.

"Chiron!" he called out. "Master Chiron!" In the distance, the centaur heard the urgency in the oarsman's voice, and slowed to a stop. He turned, raising an arm to signal acknowledgement of Phlegyas. Phlegyas scanned left and right, assuring himself no others were present, and then stepped out of his skiff, running all the way over to Chiron.

"Chiron, I have a theory of the identity of the Awakened One," he said, out of breath.

Chiron's eyes revealed his interest, "Who is the awakened prisoner, Phlegyas?"

"I believe a better question would be *what*, Lord Chiron."

Chapter 33
Rage and Pain in the Pitch

Aetos was only able to scream silently; nothing else. He was sinking in boiling, black pitch. The demons that had ravaged and abducted him and Panos dropped him into a river of sticky, boiling blackness, maintained by tall, thin creatures that ran and flew in short jerky movements like dragonflies. The beasts patrolled the boiling pitch from the shore and in the air, and were constantly looking to skewer and rip apart humans who dared expose themselves. There were many in the pitch with Aetos.

Aetos' boiling was intensified by his anger at being captured. Out of his three fellow escapees, he alone had to endure the pitch. Darius had not been captured, and Panos had fallen earlier, accidentally dropped in a higher circle where flame fell on a burning plain. Aetos could feel it while he was being dragged through the air by the flying demons, dangling at the end of their meat hooks. He could see the flame forming below before it shot to the ground. The demons had flown just above where the fiery precipitation formed, but still under the misty ceiling. Aetos saw Panos drop out of sight.

During the flight, Aetos figured out, listening to their growls and rage, the demons were arguing amongst themselves. They swore violent oaths while in the air, tossing Aetos' immobilized form about like a dead fish on their hooks. Aetos was alone, isolated far from his two fellow fugitives; the thought, a torment that worsened the effects of capture.

Aetos had been dropped from high up. The demons had removed their meat hooks from his flesh and held him by the ankles. His exposed entrails hung down, dropping across his face, evidence of the earlier violence. The demons were laughing, joking how it would surprise the 'devils' when the human fell and pushed one of them into the pitch. Aetos was not the first, nor would he be the last fugitive taken to the pitch. This was the fate of fugitives that Philo had warned the three companions about. When Aetos was at last released he plunged quickly down, landing like a load of bricks onto the back of one of the thin creatures that had been hovering over the pitch. The beast did not know what hit it.

Nearby beasts, startled by the sound of the impact of Aetos and the creature onto the pitch, began shrieking in alarm; running or flying helter skelter, not thinking to look up. This chaotic behavior gave the demons a long and hearty laugh before they flew off, looking for another round of gruesome mischief. Aetos had no way to avoid his situation; the demons had ripped through his connecting muscle and ligaments almost completely. He was on fire, in the pitch, and there was nothing he could do about it. He could only surrender his body to the downward pull of the pitch while the screeching worker beast was being pulled out by his fellows.

It was a far cry from the tedium of his safely structured Earth life with all its inherited privilege. It was also a far cry from the vile Vestibule with its constant swarm of Hell Flies. He wondered, very briefly, what it all meant.

Aetos was only able to scream silently, nothing else. He was sinking in boiling, black pitch.

AngelFall Book II

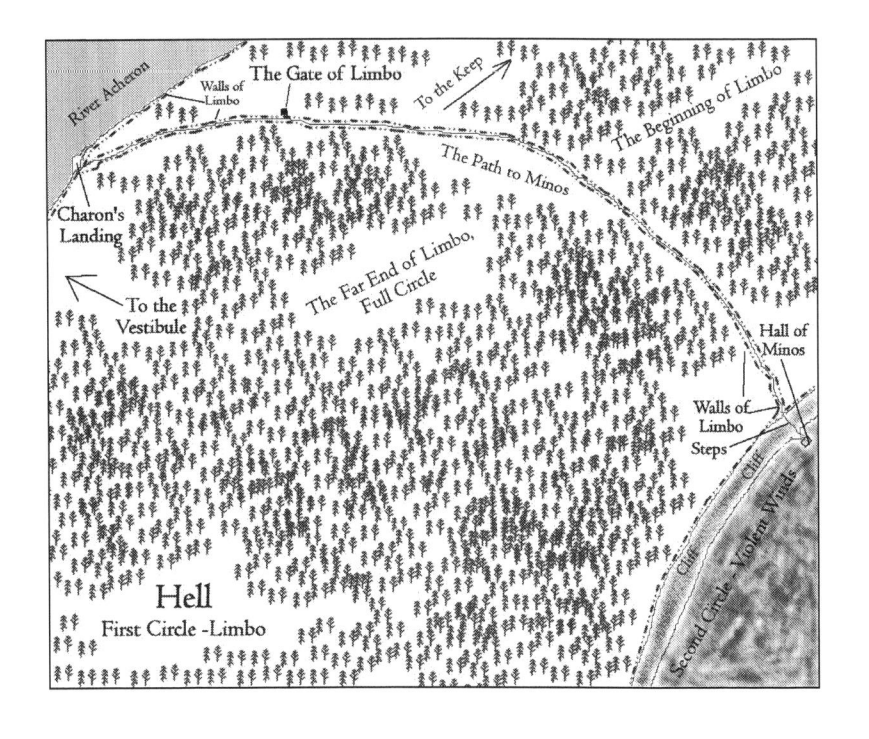

Chapter 34
The New World

Mortuus could not believe his nose. The air smelled beautiful. There was no feeling of gloom, decay or pain; hopelessness no longer weighed heavily upon him. The background noises were missing, too; the constant moaning, crying, and screaming from the depths no longer assaulted his senses. Since his awakening, he had been trying to get here. He would never leave. It was bright and colorful, and green grass grew, cooling his bare feet. Large trees and brush grew here, too.

The soldiers led Mortuus and Darius, surrounding them tightly to conceal their presence. The youthful one who introduced himself as Socius was at the head of this pack, and Mortuus, larger than any one of them, crouched in vain to conceal himself in the center. The soldiers were not pointing their weapons at Mortuus and Darius anymore.

* * * * * *

The fugitive friends had been shocked and afraid when they had been suddenly surrounded by the company of soldiers. Both thought these men were going to punish them for the incident with Charon, and turn them over to the demon fugitive hunters. When the youth, Socius, stepped up from behind the company, the soldiers lowered their weapons. Socius, introducing himself, asked Mortuus for his name. Mortuus pulled out the signed parchment of Aristotle and gave it to Socius. The youth smiled more brightly.

"I am Mortuus." replied Mortuus.

"Put your weapons away," Socius told the soldiers. He addressed Mortuus. "You were awakened by my teacher and mentor. I have much to tell you, but we must get back. The smells and sounds are unnerving my friends and myself. I now know why Aristotle would not allow me to accompany him on his journeys. He will flay me alive if he finds out I have left Limbo."

"Limbo?" said Mortuus. The boy did not hear Mortuus speak. Socius motioned the soldiers to help Mortuus to his feet. He turned toward Darius, who was staring downward sadly. Darius knew they only meant to take Mortuus, and he would soon lose his new friend.

"And who would you be?" asked Socius, peering into the hardened, weary face of Darius. The gaunt, older man looked as though he would cry. Mortuus spoke quickly.

"This is Darius. He has been helping me to get to Limbo. I arrived earlier, but was denied access. The guards were forbidden by another from within Limbo to allow me entrance. I was sent away. I crossed the river, where I met Darius. He showed me a pool where I could clean off and helped when I was attacked by the ferryman."

"Mortuus, you will have to slow down." said Socius. Mortuus' face reddened.

"That is all." said Mortuus. Socius' curiosity was peaked, but he looked confused. It was apparent that Mortuus wanted Darius to come along into Limbo. Socius knew the Elders would pick up on this, use it to cause trouble for himself and Aristotle. But the stench out here was unbearable, and the pain in Darius' face was too sad. Socius decided not to care what the Elders would do, and made up his mind. They would be dealt with later.

"Darius. You are a fugitive also?" he inquired. Darius was reluctant to answer. Socius felt his aversion to answering the question, and explained. "Darius, I am not the judge of Hell, and I do not have nor do I want the power to condemn, fugitive or not. Tell me the truth. *Are you a fugitive?*"

Darius looked downward, and sighed. He was sad and disappointed, but he would not lie to the likeable youth. "I am." Darius looked furtively around at the soldiers, who were curious to hear

Darius's response. Surprisingly, he felt no judgment from any one. He continued, "I, with two others, escaped the Hell Flies of the Vestibule, which continuously herded and pursued us, causing us to run or be bitten by the swarms. We reached a pool, that which Mortuus spoke of, where my two friends were captured by flying beasts and taken away... on the end of meat hooks." Some of the soldiers grimaced at hearing this. "I saw both creatures descending at the last possible moment, and hid myself." He looked down at the ground, his voice choking, and he spoke in a low voice, "I was a coward. When I heard my friends screaming and being ripped apart, all I could think was to hide myself." The wiry man stifled his sobs. Socius and the soldiers watched this sad spectacle.

"*I* have never had to face demons, let alone fight them Darius. Aristotle has many stories of near encounters, and each time he has thanked his lucky stars to have escaped. The demons are far too strong for any man. I am sure ten men would hardly be a match for a single beast, let alone three men to two of them. I know if your friends were here, they would join us in Limbo. Will you join us, Darius?" Darius looked up wet eyed, unsure of what he had heard; Socius smiled.

"You would permit me entrance?" asked Darius, looking around at the soldiers and then back to Socius. "Are you sure? I – "

"I would Darius; *we* would." said Socius as he looked around at the soldiers; they nodded in agreement. He looked over to Mortuus cheerily. "What do you say Mortuus, shall we have Darius accompany us to Limbo?" Mortuus smiled broadly.

"Yes! Thank you, Socius, thank you." said Mortuus. He smiled at Socius and the soldiers. "I was afraid I would have to part company with Darius."

"You are welcome Mortuus. Shall we go? It is quite awful out here." said Socius. The youth smiled and began walking down the path. Mortuus and Darius stood among the soldiers as they started walking behind Socius toward the gate. After a short walk, they arrived at the gate, a large iron door on the left side of the path. The gate was locked, and one of the soldiers knocked on the metal, banging it loudly with the haft of a long sword. Socius motioned to the soldiers.

"Remember, the Elders need not know of this. As far as they are concerned, we went on an adventure beyond the gate, just as Aristotle does, though of much lesser ambition. We have traveled even less distance than the missing three Elders. We turned back because we could not take the stench."

"Whew!" shouted one of the soldiers. "That is no lie!" The rest of the soldiers laughed. Socius resumed.

"Our new friends should be hidden from the populace until we can get them cleaned up and blend them into Limbo's citizenry. They should become indistinguishable from our fellow inhabitants. Those of you who know the guard at the inner gate will need to get his complicity. Mortuus and Darius – stay to the center; the soldiers will surround you. We can get our friends some of the waters and healing potions." He turned to Mortuus and Darius. "Please follow my directions and keep a low profile until we get you cleaned up. The politics at work here are less than benevolent, Mortuus. Be especially careful when we pass the Keep. It is the first, and worst, obstacle to your membership of Limbo. That is the castle where the Elders reside."

The guard opened the gate. Crouching slightly, Mortuus and Darius entered, surrounded on all sides by the company of soldiers. Slowly they made their way through and past the inner gate. They had made it; they were in. The company kept them pressed within as they passed the building known as the Keep, a large stone palace with many windows that fell just short of the walls in height. The Keep had five tall towers, each with four windows. A single tower in the center stood all the way up and pierced the mist. Its top could not be seen.

"Admiring the high tower, eh?" said the guard nearest to Mortuus. "That is where the Elders meet with Fallen. It is forbidden to enter without the permission of the Elders. What I would give to explore it all the way above the mist…"

The group continued to a place called the Fields of Elysius, out of eyesight of the Keep, and finally broke the tight formation. Socius left on an errand, and the soldiers, relaxed, placing their weapons down and breathing deeply, relieved to be back inside Limbo. They all sat on the grass, the smell of which made Mortuus's senses dance. A cool, gentle breeze flowed through the trees that surrounded the fields. Mortuus lay on the grass and breathed the fresh air. The soldiers smiled as they saw his childlike joy. They could not fathom what he had endured outside of these walls.

Darius, the once diligent and loyal slave remained silent, looking in awe at the brightness of the colors of everything, wondering how long his time in Limbo would last. It was brightly lit, though he could not tell from where the light came. Outer Hell was dingy and dark grey; everything seemed a shade of gray or black. Philo had said the depths were darker than the Vestibule, but he had not visited Limbo and seen its vivid hues. Darius hadn't breathed clean, fresh air for a long time. He was as overwhelmed as Mortuus looked and surprised that he might have caught a glimmer of the same insecurity he was feeling coming from his tall friend. The lifetime experience of being identified as no more than chattel had not prepared Darius to easily embrace this sort of kindness or generosity of spirit, this recognition of him as an individual. He was unworthy. He had always been unworthy from the time of his birth. And in his unworthiness, he was sure his wondrous stay would end with his eviction from Limbo. The only question was when.

The two were the center of attention, as, shyly, one of the soldiers asked a question of Mortuus. That seemed to open the floodgates for the remaining warriors. The soldiers inquired about the torments and wanderings of both Darius and Mortuus. None of them had been outside since arriving in Hell. Now they had actual inhabitants from outer Hell to ask personally. Mortuus and Darius could not have been happier to answer.

Chapter 35
Limbo's Newest Elder

Mortuus was large, with big, broad shoulders and a strong body that was wrapped in robes more refined and well-meshed than the death shrouds that covered all the new arrivals of Hell. His robes were indeed more similar to the robes of Limbo's citizens. Darius, in his ripped, stained shroud, was conspicuous as an escapee.

Two Elders, informed by a guard loyal to them about Socius and his warrior friends' exit from Limbo, went at once to Elysius, where they discovered why Socius and his warrior friends ventured outside of the gates. Raging mad, the pair began a shouting battle with Socius and Militus, who joined the group just before the pair of Elders walked onto the scene. Previously, the soldiers and Mortuus and Darius were talking amongst themselves and sharing their stories. Socius, upon seeing the Elders approach, motioned the two newcomers to be silent. Mortuus and Darius sat quietly as the fear of expulsion gnawed at them. They could not bear to consider leaving this wonderful place.

The Elders marched straight up to the group, eyeballing Mortuus and Darius disdainfully and speaking about them as if they were not present. The Elders were Alcander, one of the original Elders, and the more recently elected Morpheus. The Elder Morpheus was much taller and more stockily built than Alcander, and he moved aggressively toward Mortuus, scrutinizing him with an angry glare. Mortuus was reminded of something he had seen earlier, during his travels in the Sixth Circle, though in the moment he could not recall.

Unexpectedly, Mortuus, who was still sitting on the ground, caught sight of the Elder's form shifting from Morpheus the Elder to something not human. Mortuus, taken off guard and not entirely sure of what he was seeing blinked hard, but Morpheus, whose gaze had been locked onto the fugitive, caught Mortuus' reaction and within a split second, grabbed him by his arm and pulled his large frame to a standing position with unnatural strength.

Alcander, looking surprised, addressed Socius, attempting to distract attention from Morpheus, but it was too late for subterfuge. Socius reddened, seething with anger.

"What is the meaning of this, Socius!?!" Alcander was already bellowing with a false, pompous rage. "You went outside the gates – "

Alcander stopped mid-sentence. Morpheus was making strange, claw-like motions, as if he were trying to shred Mortuus' robes.

Mortuus was flailing, attempting to wrestle his arm from Morpheus' grip, which he could not, and protect himself from Morpheus' bizarre attack. At the same time Socius, who had instinctively grabbed for Mortuus' free arm and was pulling it in an attempt move Mortuus aside, inadvertently left Mortuus more open to Morpheus' "clawing." Mortuus' robe was beginning to tear. Instantly seeing his mistake, Socius released Mortuus, and confronted Morpheus directly.

"Let go Morpheus!" yelled Socius, intervening, but Morpheus, in a move faster than Socius could see, backhanded the youth with such force that Socius flew into a grassy mound over five meters away. His landing was padded by Darius, who had been standing close to Mortuus when the altercation began. Socius got to his feet quickly, stunned, wobbly, and in shock from the Elder's ferocious blow. Darius had the wind knocked out of him and lay on the ground, gasping for air.

Militus leapt into action. He had observed the violence with which his favorite student was struck and reckoned something extraordinary and unnatural was occurring. Despite his apprehension, Militus hoped he could interrupt the provocation before it escalated further. He barreled towards the Elder, with a running tackle that dislocated his shoulder with a loud crunch. Militus went to his knees, holding his shoulder when the Elder sent a kick that propelled him up and backward nearly as far as Socius. The Elder had been barely phased by Militus' attack. Mortuus swung at Morpheus, missing as the shifting Elder ducked.

"Get the horn, Alcander! Quickly!" shouted the Elder. Only this time, his voice was changed to low, rasping tone.

Mortuus remembered this sound and knew he was in real trouble. This was a demon, like the one he had seen in the tomb area, but somehow transformed. Morpheus grabbed Mortuus by his neck one-handed; he was growling and sneering. His facade now barely stable, he pulled Mortuus' head down and rasped intimately, "You will wish you had never awakened from your eternal sleep!"

Mortuus was choking in the iron grip of the masquerading beast. Out of desperation, he grabbed the offending hand causing his distress and pulled the fingers back, breaking them like dry twigs. The creature screeched in surprised rage and retracted its broken left hand, instantly swinging at Mortuus with it's right and causing a shallow, long gash to appear on his left cheek. Mortuus, emboldened by the way he was able to easily break the digits of the beast, swung hard, connecting his fist to the creature's chin. The demon elder fell backward with a heavy thud against a nearby tree trunk. It hissed at Mortuus in a way that left no doubt as to his true identity. Now everyone watching was aware Morpheus was a demon.

Alcander was beside himself. His anger at Socius was replaced by his fear at the untimely revelation that Morpheus was a demon. A demon had been in the midst of the Elders! How had this happened?

"Wait, stop, all of you. Stop, stop, by the Gods!" yelled Alcander, looking around nervously. Everyone was still; shocked in place. Their eyes were following Morpheus who had begun inching his way towards Mortuus, hissing and crouched like a hungry, wild animal stalking it's prey. The crowd was building, yet no one could be distracted from the scene before them.

"Morpheus! Stop this now!" pleaded a now sweating Alcander.

All eyes were on Morpheus, the Elder, who was growling like a feral beast at the giant fugitive. Mortuus stared back, preparing himself for battle. The warriors, at a gesture from Militus, made a semi-circle around Mortuus, Socius and Darius, and brandished their weapons; unnerved by this first time confrontation with a demon. The tense sensation of real, serious battle had not been felt by any of them in centuries

"Fugitives! You will be tormented far worse than your sentence. I will see to it. The pitch awaits you!" snarled the demon Elder as he looked past the guards, focusing only on Mortuus. "Warrior fools, you shall share their fate for your insolence!"

"What sort of Elder are you, Morpheus?" challenged Mortuus, "These people already know you are not human. Why don't you show them your true form; the one I see before me?"

Morpheus roared like an ensnared animal, but deeply and with uncanny resonance.

"Demon!" shouted Mortuus, calling the beast out, "You have no authority in this place; you belong here no more than Plutus!"

Morpheus snarled back his reply. "I am sent by the Masters to watch these humans. You cannot escape the wrath of the Masters, and you will not escape me."

In a sudden upward bound, the creature was revealed. His form changing dramatically as he became a flyer demon, with great wings suddenly appearing behind him and bearing him straight up into the air and away from the warriors. Downward, floating, then falling, came his robes, thrown from his form as he transfigured. The crowd beyond the soldiers gasped.

"No wonder," thought Militus as he held his throbbing shoulder. The revered old warrior shouted to his men, commanding them to engage the flying beast. The warriors raised their spears, and bent their bows, but before any shot could fly, Morpheus was gone, vanishing into the misty heights. The demon's speed was faster than they could target.

Militus, in pain, rushed at a nearby tree and slammed it with his dislocated shoulder. He groaned as his shoulder pressed back into the socket. The crowding spectators, growing more numerous, started to talk amongst themselves, and in moments they turned on Alcander, shouting oaths about his treachery, allowing demons into their governance, and some began demanding to know where the missing Elders were, and why had he taken part in the conspiracy to remove them. Alcander was crushed by their comments, red in the face with embarrassment and his inability to control the crowd. Militus had some difficulty silencing them but it was imperative to get the situation under control:

"Please everyone! We will address this situation. Please, let's quiet down," yelled Militus. The crowd, many of them warriors, became silent. Mortuus, discovered, was full of thoughts of expulsion from

Limbo. He distracted himself by tending to his facial wounds, wiping the blood from his body with his robes. Darius was also preparing himself for his imminent exile to outer Hell.

"Thanks all, for your peace. At this time, I would address Alcander now. Alcander? Alcander! Come back here!" yelled Militus.

Alcander was on the move, afraid of the enraged crowd. Several soldiers ran after him, tackling him to the ground. They carried him back before the crowd, kicking and screaming.

"Put me down! Put me down! I did not know! I did not know!" screamed the pot bellied elder as they placed his feet on the grass, but held on to his shoulders and arms. He was desperate, frantic. Socius came up to him, looking him squarely in the face. "Socius, you believe me don't you? Please, tell them! Socius –"

Socius stopped Alcander's words with a wave of his hand, and Militus spoke.

"Alcander. You have brought a demon among us! A *demon*, Alcander! And you complain about two simple fugitives? What madness is this!?" Militus looked at Alcander's profusely sweating face.

"I did not know, Militus. I swear to you I did not –"

Alcander's attention was suddenly engaged by something above; his eyes were widening in fear. Socius and the others followed his gaze to the demon Morpheus, who was flying overhead and descending fast. Morpheus landed near Mortuus and the surrounding warriors. Murmuring inarticulately, he motioned his left arm and the warriors who wielded their weaponry flew backward as if hit by an invisible force field. They landed harshly, each dazed. Socius was readying to attack, and Militus reached for a spear on the ground with his good arm, keeping his eyes on the demon Elder.

"Do not move, any of you, or I will flay you before I drop you into the pitch." He turned toward Mortuus and hissed; long rows of fangs bared in his wide open mouth. "You will come with me now or I will make your punishment far worse than what awaits you!"

Mortuus, expecting to be given up by the crowd appeared sad and defeated. He did not wish to have his friends sent to torment. Now they would suffer for helping him, for allowing him into Limbo. At worst, he had expected only to be exiled. Never did it occur to him the good and kindly warriors, and Socius, would suffer.

"You have enjoyed your stay here in Limbo, then?" taunted the rasping demon, smiling hideously in derision. It's eyes were dark black, with thin red veins webbing around the interior as though holding the eyeball in place.

Mortuus's face dropped, and Socius, seeing his friend in such emotional pain, struggled to find a way out of the situation. The demon continued his jeering, moving closer to Mortuus.

"You will come with m-"

That was the end of the demon's cruel taunts. Mortuus struck the beast squarely in the face, causing it to crumple into a heap. Militus looked in stunned disbelief. The shock of the sight caused the crowd to freeze. From the back, one voice shouted.

"He beat the demon!"

But the demon slowly staggered to his feet and in a daze, moved toward Mortuus slowly.

"Hit it! Hit it again!" yelled another voice. And soon, most of the crowd, along with the warriors, was cheering Mortuus on.

Mortuus struck again and the crowd cheered.

Morpheus staggering, his wings beginning to stretch out slowly, involuntarily, stared at the ground as he fought to remain on his feet. Seizing the moment, Mortuus grabbed a wing of the demon, wrapping his free arm around its neck; he constricted the creature's throat with all his might. The beast struggled desperately, doing everything in its power to rid itself of Mortuus' grasp, but it was obvious he had been weakened considerably by the stranger's two blows.

Mortuus released the wing, and forced the demon's head forward, placing him in a choke hold that would have crushed the throat and neck bones of a human.

The demon thrashed violently, falling onto the ground and rolling over on its back like it was on fire; Mortuus would not relent. After that brief struggle, it managed to get back to its feet, and crashed Mortuus against the nearby trees; Mortuus hung on with growing strength. For the spectators, it was all they could do to stay out of the way of the titanic struggle. Alcander paled; Socius barred his way many times when the Elder tried to slip away from the scene. New spectators arrived, not understanding what was happening, but attracted by the noise of the crowd.

The beast continued to claw and gouge the arms and body of Mortuus in his attempts to free himself, but after awhile, it finally began slowing down, dropping to its knees. Its flapping wings suddenly vanished into its back, disappearing, as if into thin air, retracted in the purple-tinged skin of the demon. With a final push backwards, both men fell, Mortuus underneath, holding onto the demon's neck as if he would wrench it off. The demon's arms, still clutching the forearm of Mortuus, fell limp to its sides and lay on the ground; its dark eyes rolled up into its head. All was silent.

Socius and Militus moved forward cautiously as Mortuus kept his stranglehold firm.

"Mortuus. Mortuus." Said Socius. "I believe the creature is dead. I you think you can let go."

Militus also spoke, looking at the pair on the ground. It appeared to him that Mortuus had a stranglehold on a corpse. Militus kicked at the creature's legs, not really wanting to check its eyes, and getting no involuntary response he declared,

"I think it is dead, Mortuus. Why don't you let go? We -"

Before Militus could finish his sentence, a loud explosion, and a large amount of dark black smoke lay atop Mortuus, exactly in the space where the demon Morpheus had been. Mortuus lay on the ground, choking on the smoke, his back and forearms scratched and ripped, bleeding profusely. He coughed as he gasped for air and found only smoke. Socius and Militus fanned away the black smoke and picked him up by his arms. The warriors came forward with a look of awe, clapping him on the shoulders and back. Alcander, who was trying to slip away again, was grabbed by two of the warriors.

The gathered crowd, standing in disbelief, broke out at once, cheering, whooping and hollering at the demise of a real demon. Everyone wanted to get closer to Mortuus. Darius moved near to his friend, taking the Mortuus' arm from Militus, who was still nursing his sore shoulder. Socius spoke to the overjoyed crowd.

"Mortuus, the Demon Slayer!" he exclaimed exuberantly as he held up the bloodied arm of Mortuus.

He wanted to celebrate this victory -- the likes of which had never been seen in Limbo -- as loudly and as exuberantly as he could. Excitement was abounding through him and the crowd, a high never before felt in this reality. The crowd returned his joyous exuberance before Militus moved toward the youth.

"Socius," Militus interrupted, looking serious, "We must go."

Socius could see the serious look in his eyes. Turning to the soldiers, Militus began mobilizing, "We need to help our hero, men. Have any of you vials from the three waters, regeneration accelerators, or any fruits? Give some to Mortuus - as we walk. We must hide him...you men," Militus waved to a small company nearby, "disperse the crowd. We need as little attention as possible."

"What? But, why? What is wrong, Militus?" asked Socius. "We should celebrate this moment!"

"Socius, hear me. We must go now!" said Militus, deadly solemn. "This demon worked directly for the Fallen. There will be trouble, and soon."

Socius nodded his head, chagrined at the folly of his youthful exuberance. Militus was right. What repercussions would come were wholly unknown – nothing this big had ever happened before in Limbo. They must move, and move *now*. Militus looked at the men holding onto Alcander and scowled slightly.

"Bring the bureaucrat."

"Where will we go?" asked Socius. "Limbo is large, though quite finite for flying creatures and Fallen."

Just then, a medium built, cloaked figure, who had been standing in the back of the crowd, stepped forward.

"Go to the Hall of Science – they can help you."

Militus nodded his head in agreement, then gestured to a man, an ogre-ish, older warrior type who stood near the cloaked figure. The ogre-man tapped the cloaked man on the left shoulder and then grabbed him by the scruff of the neck. pushing him toward the front of the crowd roughly. Militus and Socius lifted the stranger's hood revealing a curly topped young man with pale skin, a chiseled face and bright, intelligent eyes.

"Barak!" they exclaimed synchronously.

Barak was a student of the Chronicler, the chief Historian, and the Chronicler was the oldest known resident of Limbo; a legend who was highly respected and venerated, especially by the scientists. He had witnessed Limbo change from its dark, barren landscape into the current beautiful haven. The Hall of Science even had a statue depicting the Chronicler, though very few people actually knew what he looked like. Barak was his best known student because he often traveled back and forth from the Chronicler's homestead, near Basel, almost full circle from the gate of Limbo, to the Hall of Science and the Great Library. He was a friendly sort, sharing the teachings he learned from the Chronicler and always eager to discuss the known and unknown origins of Limbo and Hell itself with a willing listener.

"Greetings old friends. It has been a long time." said Barak. He turned to face Mortuus, who was examining his wounds after drinking several vials of the waters, happily given to him by assorted warriors and members of the crowd. Mortuus, though bleeding and in pain, was enjoying the water immensely. He shared a few vials with Darius, telling him these were what he had been talking of earlier when they were at the rocky oasis.

"Take these, demon slayer." said Barak, smiling, as he held out four small, blue fruits for Mortuus. "They are from the orchards between Terni and Porto, a long walk from here. Though not as fresh as when I picked them, they will still speed your healing greatly." Mortuus took the fruits, examining them curiously, and offered his thanks. He handed two to Darius, who didn't really need them and handed them back laughing.

"I think you need these more than me, friend."

"Fellows," Barak announced loudly, "You should get to the Hall of Science. There is much to learn about a newcomer who can slay a demon with his bare hands. And there will be trouble, I am afraid." He dropped his voice to address Mortuus. "You can remain in Limbo, Mortuus, but you must go now despite your injuries. Those fruits will accelerate your regeneration." Finally, as though checking off a list that he held in his head, Barak turned to Militus,

"Militus, I am returning to the Chronicler's cottage, and will walk with you. They will need to wash and get new robes, they carry the scent of outer Hell. Incidentally, how did you manage to get two fugitives past the Elders' guards?" asked Barak.

"It was the boy," deadpanned Militus, "Socius is blossoming into either a great leader or a juvenile delinquent." Barak smiled, as did Socius.

The group began their walk deeper into Limbo, much to the joy of Mortuus and Darius. Mortuus had been certain the fight would be the last of his time inside Limbo's gate. Darius was convinced likewise, that their moment of bliss was nearly over. But now they were headed farther within the landscape. Quietly, both walked and took in the peaceful scenery, trying to make it last as long as it possibly could.

Militus left a small company of soldiers at the fields, with two men designated to be runners; if there was trouble, one of them could be dispatched to warn the traveling party. Ten soldiers accompanied, two of whom forcibly escorted Alcander. The pair of fugitives walked and ate the small fruits they had been given. Mortuus sighed contentedly, unaware of how everyone was studying him as they walked; each proud to be near the mighty demon slayer and more proud that they had trusted their friend Socius to venture out the gate. It had been a day of daring and adventure for them all.

A small subset of the crowd stayed in the fields, talking excitedly about the events they had just beheld. Adventure had come directly to them; true excitement that they had never before or ever after would expect to see again. Oft times, all had shared stories of adventure and daring. Most were from moments of their lives. None had ever, in their lives or in the afterlife, come close to what they had just observed.

Now, in Limbo, the greatest story ever told would be, 'Mortuus the Demon Slayer.'

And it had occurred right before their eyes.

Chapter 36
The Walk to Bremen

It was a long walk to Bremen, a tiny village where the Hall of Science protruded up from its center, its four stories dwarfing the surrounding small huts and cottages. The path had started euphorically for Mortuus and Darius. Each had enjoyed the fruits provided by Barak, and everyone was abuzz with Mortuus' victory over the demon Elder. Everyone except, of course, Alcander, who was prodded along by his two guards; Alcander spent most of the time trying to explain that he had no idea Morpheus was a demon. Militus was so angry that he threatened to gag the ranting Alcander until they reached Bremen. To the great relief of all, Alcander finally conceded and remained quiet.

The soldiers who were escorting the group continued to ask question after question of Mortuus. All wanted to congratulate Mortuus on his victory, and they invited him to partake of their battle games, should he feel up to it at a later time. Mortuus replied that he had had all the battle games he could take outside the walls of Limbo, but he did thank them for their offer, saying it was an honor to be asked.

Socius filled in Mortuus and Darius about Benjamin. Benjamin was the chief scientist of Limbo, and had worked in the Hall of Science for many centuries. The Hall of Science was responsible for all of the agricultural and manufacturing development and processing. Benjamin, ever curious and always tinkering, had overseen many of the initial developments which led to making Limbo the green, beautiful countryside it had become; he was renowned for his work.

"Agriculture?" asked Darius. "What need have they here for growing foods in a large scale?"

"Not just foods," replied Socius, "but plants for dyes and regeneratives, and of course, wines. Some here have quite a taste for the foods, even though they do not hunger. It reminds them of their lives, mostly, and makes them feel normal. I, having been raised here, actually do hunger."

"That is a slight understatement," Militus chimed in jokingly. "The boy can eat! His appetite is legendary!" Barak laughed loudly at this.

"He is a growing boy, Militus," added Barak. "No others have ever grown here. Socius is truly one of the many wonders of Hell."

"What of earlier times?" asked Mortuus. "What existed here before the Hall of Science came to be?"

Militus answered, "It was darker, Mortuus. And these walls did not exist."

Mortuus looked at the walls to his left and right. They were never far out of sight unless the group passed through a well treed section of path, but even then there were always peepholes that revealed more walls. It was a constant reminder to Mortuus that Hell was never far away.

"When I first arrived, there was little to separate us from the outside," continued Militus, "The only benefit to being placed in Limbo was that we were not tormented. We could talk with each other, but always to the background noise and odor of Hell."

"How did you get the walls built? They are so high." said Mortuus.

"When the first plants and trees were developed by the scientists and then cultivated successfully, the Fallen erected the walls." said Militus. " In a matter of days, the walls, as you see them, were constructed. We saw no Fallen, nor any of their workers, perform the magic required to build anything so large, but we do know where they got the rock. Strangely, no one witnessed the construction either; we are certain it was Fallen magic. The scientists believe that the Fallen wished to contain the plants we had cultivated within Limbo. They believe the Fallen do not want to even allow a glimmer of hope to the damned."

"What do you mean, Militus?" asked Mortuus.

"The plants and trees here grow very quickly. Do you not enjoy their beauty?" asked Militus.

"I do. And if I understand your meaning," replied Mortuus, "Hell would not be a proper place of torment with beautiful plants and trees growing everywhere. The Fallen magic must be very powerful to achieve such great feats of architecture. Did they also build the Great Library and the Hall of Science?"

"No," answered Militus, "The Fallen do not care for our scientific or educational progress. We have much time on our hands, and so we are able to do quite a bit of building. The walls are the only gifts from the Fallen. They also keep out the fugitives. Once the walls were in place, the odors and sounds diminished; more so as we cultivated greater areas of Limbo. Did you notice the freshness of the air when you entered the gate?"

"Yes. I enjoyed the air more than I can say, Militus. I am still enjoying it. How does Limbo have this brightness? I see no source of light. Outer hell is only gray, or black and white."

"I can help answer your question." Barak interjected, "The plant from which most of the other plant life was developed actually glows from within itself. I do not recall the name of the plant, but the glow is very strong. It is believed the plant was discovered by the Chronicler himself and given to the scientists."

"Your curiosity is refreshing, Mortuus." said Militus. "You can get many questions answered better by Benjamin. He is an odd fellow, very quirky and very smart."

The group continued walking for some time before anyone spoke again. This time it was Socius who started the conversation.

"Darius, do you have any idea where your friends were taken to? Did the demons speak before they took Panos and Aetos?" said the youth.

"I was hidden in such a way that I could not overhear any of their conversation. It was all rasping and growls only." said Darius. But before we escaped from the torment of the Hell Flies, we spoke with another who had escaped and had been captured. His name was Philo. Philo, knowing we contemplated escape, repeatedly told us the fate of all fugitives is in the boiling pitch of the Eighth Circle. He somehow managed to escape the pitch and return to the Vestibule, swearing he would not ever attempt escape again. He warned us many times before our flight from the Hell Fly captivity."

"Your fate is the same, Darius." warned Alcander, a smug priggishness. "You should have listened to Philo."

"Still your tongue, fool Elder." snapped Militus. "Or I will cut it out."

"You too, Militus," the pot-bellied bureaucrat sneered, "In fact, all of you will share it. Aristotle already knows of what I speak. He disregarded our advice for the last time!" Alcander, used to his Elder's privilege for too long, forgot his place and was not aware at first of what he had revealed.

"What do you mean?" said Socius, who stepped directly in front of Alcander. "Tell me now, Alcander."

Alcander realizing suddenly what he had just said, clamped up, and did not elaborate. He choked and stumbled on his words, attempting to lie at first, then trying to take back his statement as the group closed in, curious and angry at his treachery.

"Aristotle has been taken." admitted Alcander weakly. "He would not listen to reason." Alcander hung his head, as if in defeat. "There is no coming back. The Fallen were very angry that Aristotle had been wandering for so long a time." And with that, silence ensued for a short while.

Thus, the trip to Bremen, which started happily, ended in mourning. Socius, beside himself with grief, walked away from the group and stood near a tree with his head down, shoulders trembling slightly. Everyone waited and watched sadly as his inconsolable anguish released itself in quiet paroxysms of despair. It had been hundreds of years and Socius never imagined he could lose the closest person to him. He had to reach for the tree to support himself when his legs began giving way. Everyone remained quiet until Socius returned. Militus, another father figure to Socius, stared helplessly, heartbroken at the great loss to this centuries-old youth. Militus had thought Aristotle a fool for his wanderings outside of Limbo, but he did respect the care and love that Aristotle provided in the upbringing of this most beloved student. What would the boy do now?

Aristotle was lost forever.

Chapter 37
Meeting Benjamin

They arrived in a field just outside of Bremen many hours later, still reeling from the revelation of Aristotle's abduction by the Fallen and their demons. The field would be a better location, according to Militus, as they would need to be as discrete as possible for the sake of Mortuus and Darius. The pair of newcomers still wore their ripped and stained clothing, and would stand out greatly against the common garb of the people of Limbo.

Militus left them and went to find the senior scientist, Benjamin. Socius kept to himself, unwilling to be consoled by the others. Alcander was laid down on the field by the guards that had carried him. Since the revelation concerning his awareness of and apparent collusion in Aristotle's capture, Alcander had been incapacitated, unable to keep up with the pace of the group. His face was bruised badly, his jaw broken, and he still spat out blood and teeth from the severe beating that Socius had given him. In the end, no one could pull Socius off of Alcander except Mortuus. Alcander had been screaming through most of the onslaught. Now he lay on the field, broken and injured. The guards had been careful to keep him far from Socius, who sat and stared into the forest surrounding the field. Mortuus and Darius sat with the soldiers and Barak.

"You will like the scientist," said Barak, addressing Mortuus and Darius. "He is the one to direct all of your questions."

"Why is it that we are meeting the scientist?" asked Mortuus.

"You have *slain* a true demon," answered Barak, "Something we did not know to be possible; and along with the mystery of your strange origin, it becomes more apparent that you were being hidden for a reason. We need to find that reason; what if your concealment was because you are a threat to the Fallen? We believe the scientist may have some idea of your identity. I am certain he will be very excited to meet with you."

Mortuus contemplated everything Barak was saying, but was doubtful. "How is it possible for me to be a threat to the Fallen, Barak?" he asked. "I beat the demon, but barely."

"You have been unconscious for many years, Mortuus. You have barely awoken, yet you had enough strength to best the demon. And, not just any demon; Morpheus was a high demon, one of the most powerful that exists. He was a magic user, so we know he has intelligence and great strength. You saw what happened when Militus tackled him." Mortuus nodded, recalling the demon's near indifference to the running tackle against him that dislocated Militus' shoulder.

"I look forward to meeting your scientist, Barak." said Mortuus.

Just as he spoke, Militus returned from the path into Bremen. At his side was a strangely built man who walked oddly, his head slightly forward of his upper body. His eyes bulged outward from his head, and he examined each person in the group, scanning. His nose, rather large and pointed, began twitching as he sniffed the air around the group.

"My friends." said Militus. "Allow me to introduce you to Benjamin." The strange man nodded to everyone, and looked across the field at Socius and further away at the recovering Alcander.

"Why is Socius sitting by himself, Militus?" asked the scientist. "And is that Alcander, the Elder, lying out over there?"

"Socius needs some time to himself for now, Benjamin. And yes, that is Alcander."

"He appears to need some regeneratives.' said Benjamin. "I can go to my hut and –"

"Do not concern yourself with Alcander, Benjamin. I will fill you in later. We need to ask you about our two new arrivals." He pointed to Mortuus and Darius and introduced each.

The pair smiled at the quirky scientist, who sniffed the air again.

"You are fugitives?" asked Benjamin. Mortuus nodded, uncomfortably.

"Militus, we must get these two washed up. They stink of outer Hell." said Benjamin. "Let us go to the First Waters. They can drink and cleanse themselves. We will take the path around Bremen. Once they are properly dressed and washed, no one will suspect their origins."

As they made ready to head toward the First Waters, Benjamin queried, "I am very curious as to why you have brought fugitives into Limbo, Militus. I know you do not approve of Aristotle's venturing outside."

"Shhh, Benjamin." whispered Militus. "I will explain as we walk. Please, do not speak Aristotle's name again." Benjamin, surprised, looked inquisitively at Militus.

They walked to the First Waters and along the way Militus quietly filled him in on Aristotle's capture, and Alcander's beating by Socius.

Mortuus and Darius, passing through the path against the wall, saw the towering building of the Hall of Science jutting high into the air and slowed to a halt, awestruck. Barak chuckled, enjoying their reactions to this architectural wonder and recalling his own amazement long ago, on his first encounter with the magnificent building.

They arrived at the First Waters following a few hours of walk. All were tired except for Mortuus and Darius, who continued to take in the splendor of Limbo, enjoying each moment. Neither had been there long enough to take any of the scenery for granted.

The First Waters was a large pool of water, flowing out of a rock face. The rock, the size of a small cottage, was partially covered in a greenish hue where the water touched it. The water moved quickly, and the swirls and eddy's of the pool flowed in the same direction as the group. Mortuus, compelled by the beauty of the clear flowing stream, walked right up to the edge, wondering if this was the same water as was in the vials. One of the soldiers told Mortuus to drink his fill; the water in the vials was indeed the same, but straight from the source it would be far more delicious. Mortuus needed no convincing. He lay on his chest and drank deeply, beyond his needs. Benjamin and Militus stopped walking and turned to watch.

Mortuus finally turned over, and lay on the bank. He was overfull, but did not wish to leave. His awakening had been a Hellish nightmare of deep dehydration. Were it not for Aristotle's vials, he would have failed to make it to Limbo.

"Mortuus, we must go to the far end of the water." said Militus. "You and Darius will need to wash there. The current is much too dangerous here."

Mortuus, feeling stronger and more vital, stood up and followed. They walked along the edge of the water for another hour or so before reaching a quiet pool. The water flowed into another rock face, filtering between stones and small boulders and disappearing underground. This, explained Barak, was the end of the First Waters.

Benjamin encouraged the pair of fugitives to wash themselves in the pool. It was very cold, but felt even better than the pool within the rocky oasis of the Vestibule. Socius, who had been following silently behind the group, also disrobed and entered the cool water, diving into the deepest part of the pool. It helped to revive his spirits, and Benjamin, now aware of Aristotle's predicament, felt it to be a good sign.

Militus set the soldiers to guarding the paths into and out of the area. He wanted to have no interruptions or surprises while they consulted Benjamin. Alcander was taken to a nearby wooded area to be concealed for the duration of their meeting.

The pair finished their swim, feeling the most alive either had since being in Hell. Benjamin, Militus and Barak were sitting on a circle of mossy boulders, waiting as they dressed. Socius came out shortly after, and joined the circle along with Mortuus and Darius.

Benjamin began the discussion.

"My friends, I have heard most of your stories from Militus and Barak as you swam. It seems that Aristotle has awakened a giant, so to speak. Mortuus, do you recall anything of your former life before the sleep?" Mortuus shook his head as he answered.

"I recall nothing. It is as if I have been born as you see me, for I have no recollection of a living life." said Mortuus. "I have feelings sometimes, but nothing to attach them to."

"You will need to regenerate for a much longer time before your memories return." said Benjamin. "I was studying the sample vial of the green liquid you and the others were force-fed; your benefactor delivered a vial of it to me by way of Socius after he returned from waking you. I believe that it was what kept you and your fellows in the sleep, and most likely also had a hand in erasing your memories."

"Have you completed your study of the liquid then, Benjamin?" asked Socius.

"I'm afraid not, Socius, the vial disappeared from my lab without a trace before I finished my analysis. Based on the log of Aristotle, however, I can well conclude what the fluid did. I also was able to discern an herb, discovered and brought to me by Aristotle that is known to slow regeneration; it grows along the edge of the Styx. It has a strong, unique odor when dried and ground. I believe the other components probably destroyed memories and kept you asleep, then this herb inhibited your brain from regenerating, thus enhancing the effects of the other components."

"But how did your sample disappear Benjamin?" asked Socius. "Are the assistants and other scientists not trustworthy?"

"I have my suspicions, Socius. There is another reason I did not bring you all into Bremen and the Hall of Science. But I will work that out myself. Now on to my next question. I have heard a commotion that something happened in Elysius recently. Would that be –"

"Mortuus destroyed a demon, Benjamin!" blurted Socius.

Benjamin studied Mortuus, his eyes scanning, searching his face.

"A demon? You destroyed one of them?" asked an incredulous Benjamin. "Was it a flyer, one of the smithies from the whirlpool area?"

"No. This one was disguised as an Elder." said Barak. That is why we brought along Alcander." Alcander was with the beast when it was found out by Mortuus. Mortuus saw right through the magic before any of us suspected."

"You saw through it? Is this verifiable, Militus?" asked Benjamin, growing more skeptical. "I would prefer more verif-"

"I saw it myself." said Militus. "Do you see my shoulder? I struck the beast with a running blow. It was as if I had charged against the boulder I sit upon. Socius and Darius were also witness to it, along with my men, who now watch the paths."

"Oh my. Oh no." said Benjamin, weakly. His face had turned a pale white. "They can change form? Then we are being infiltrated by the beasts. They will seek you as soon as they discover your absence, Mortuus. Oh my. They are among us." Benjamin's look of worry was infectious; the whole circle sat, grim-faced, looking at each other, no one knowing what to say.

'Why did no one tell me this as we walked?" asked the scientist. "The most famous event of our after-lives and you all held your tongues? No wonder your soldiers were so talkative the whole way. I should have walked along with them!"

"Things were still…delicate…after Alcander's revelation." said Barak warily. Militus nodded in agreement. Benjamin looked at Socius, who appeared somber-faced again, then decided to discontinue pursuing the subject.

"Mortuus, you must be taken to the Chronicler, but I would first have you meet Clavius." said Benjamin.

"Clavius?" uttered Socius. "Why Clavius? Where does he reside these days?"

"Clavius will test Mortuus." said Benjamin. "If Mortuus passes the test, and I am sure he will, Clavius will take him to the Chronicler. We are in dangerous times, and I believe I must go back to the Hall of Science and get some things. I realize you are skeptical, Militus, but I believe the time is nearing."

"You cannot be serious, Benjamin," replied Militus.

"Look at the signs, Militus," said Barak. "Demons living among us? Mortuus destroying one barehanded? What more do you require?"

"But where will we go? There is no escaping Hell," countered Militus, obviously troubled.

"Ahhh, yes. That has been the prevailing wisdom for thousands of years…" Benjamin, sniffing the air, blinked a couple of times looking upwards at nothing anyone else could see and continued, "But for those same thousands of years it was also 'true' that there were no beings who could destroy a demon barehanded either, Militus."

"Do your eyes lie to you?" Barak intervened, "You claim to be a witness. How come the demon did not use his magic on Mortuus as it did your soldiers?" Barak was recalling how the demon Morpheus cast a single spell that sent the soldiers flying backward. Militus grimaced.

"The demon could have cast that spell and many others upon Mortuus," advised Barak. It would not have worked. It knew this."

Worry swept across the General's face.

"Very well. I believe this may be the timing," conceded Militus. "But I do not know if we are prepared or if I am the best leader."

"You are the best we have, Militus, a noble and worthy leader, and all your men would follow you into the depths of Hell. The signs are here; we have been complacent long enough. The time to leave Hell is approaching." Benjamin turned to the group, resolved and with an assured authority in his voice.

"My friends, you must go now to Porto. Barak, take them to Clavius, and get them new robes. Stop by the Second Waters, carefully, and have them drink also. Now you must go."

And to Militus, "Gather your men, Militus. I would have you escort me to the Hall in Bremen." Nodding in the direction of Socius, Barak, Mortuus and Darius, "These four will travel alone; a small group will draw much less attention. Have your men bring Alcander also. We may have need of him."

To the four, Benjamin was somber but positive, "My friends, goodbye for now, until we meet again."

Militus whistled, and his soldiers returned within a few moments. He and the soldiers said their goodbyes to Barak, Socius, Darius and Mortuus, then ran to catch up with Benjamin, who was already far up the path. Alcander and his two guards followed the pack slowly.

"My god." said Barak. "I have never seen Benjamin this excited before. He is right; we must be on our way." The four began their trek to Porto, to meet Clavius, and then the Chronicler. They walked along in silence until Mortuus could stand it no more.

"Did he say *leave* Hell?" asked Mortuus.

Chapter 38
Panos On Fire

Panos lay writhing on the burning sand. His intestines and entrails had been ripped out of him, and lay beside him, baked dry in the oven-heat of this flat plain, until he had enough strength to gather and pull them back into his exposed abdomen. It was a slow process; the heat of the sand was intense enough to brown his back and sides where he had landed. On occasion, a falling ball of flame would strike his body, causing him to scream outright despite his lack of energy. The flame burned brightly for a few moments, and then hissed out, seeming to mock Panos's shrieks.

All around, Panos saw groups of people running across the plain, sometimes coming up close to him in their curiosity, but never staying long. They were naked, or only in blackened shards of clothing, always almost bare and blistered. They would run and rejoin their pack in short order, lifting their feet in an absurd dance to gain a moment from the intense burning. One passing man of small, thin frame yelled at him, requesting to know why he was here and how he had fallen from the sky. Apparently there were witnesses who saw the demons drop him. Panos had fully expected the demons to come back for him. When they did not, he was as relieved as a person being roasted on a burning bed of sand could be.

Many hours went by before Panos was able to sit up. The sand clung, sticking to his melted skin, and continued to burn until Panos could brush it off. As he did so well in his life as a traveler, Panos was looking around trying to orient himself to the environment. As far as he could see in the heat-distorted landscape, there was only sand and random falling flame. Knowing his pain would be reduced if he was on his feet, Panos stood up. His right leg, not fully mended from the fall, gave a loud snap, and Panos dropped with a yell to the burning sandy floor. He lay writhing again.

In his life, he had once journeyed across a great desert with nomadic traders, one of his many traveling adventures. He remembered thinking on his trip that Hell could not be any hotter. He snickered to himself, though his face and body showed no signs of snickering. "I guess I was wrong," he thought.

He had to move. He knew it was the only way, so conjuring all his willpower, Panos began to roll and crawl like an oddly cocooned worm, turning his lean body over, and side to side, to permit temporary relief in the worst burnt areas. He needed to get off of this burning desert. But how?

One of the groups passed near him. The skinny man yelled out again.

"Get to the rill! It is ahead, far in front of us. Get to the rill!" The man's voice trailed off as the frail, burnt man, pointing into the distance ahead, was gone with his group. Panos began dragging himself in the direction of the group, wincing in pain.

He would get to the rill.

Chapter 39
The Miners of the Pit

"Socius, why would Benjamin speak of leaving this place?" asked Mortuus. The group, currently composed of Darius, Socius, Mortuus, and Barak, had just left the First Waters, and was proceeding toward Graz, the next small village clockwise in the circle Limbo occupied.

"I don't know Mortuus," answered the youth, "Benjamin is privy to many bits of knowledge of which I am ignorant, and this news is impossible to me as well. I have only left Limbo once, and that was to retrieve you. We almost returned without you; once beyond the gate we became almost paralyzed by the sounds and odor of Outer Hell."

"You would not want to leave after having been outside these walls. I am most grateful to Aristotle for awakening me, but I don't know that I would have ventured outside the gate, as he did." Mortuus shook his head pensively.

Socius had considered leaving with Aristotle to journey around on many occasions. Aristotle always abruptly dismissed Socius' requests. After his short departure from Limbo to retrieve Mortuus, Socius understood. Aristotle would sometimes answer "when you are ready, only a few thousand years more." And no one else in Limbo would even entertain Socius' suggestions on the matter.

"I requested to journey with Aristotle many times, Mortuus. He always refused me, and though I argued the point, he would not be persuaded." Socius was seized with sadness as the memory of his teacher in torment forever surfaced again; his face could not hide his feelings. "I'm not sure what I will do, now that he is gone forever."

"The demon spoke of the pitch, as have you Darius." said Mortuus. "Where is this area? Has Aristotle ever visited it in his explorations?"

"The pitch is said to be in the Eighth Circle." replied Barak.

"Aristotle was never able to travel beyond the Seventh Circle," Socius explained, "It is said to be occupied by the worst of Hell's workers, and a giant flying beast who patrols the outer wall and rim." Socius, pain on his face, trailed off. He was growing sadder as they spoke of Aristotle; Mortuus discontinued any further inquiries, and the group continued walking.

The landscape became abruptly rocky and uneven, although it remained green in small patches, where grasses found small holes and cracks of soil. Brightly colored lichens grew on boulders and strips of rock. The rockiness stretched on for awhile, and though the rock coloring was dark, the landscape was unusually brightly lit. The terrain gradually became more boulder-strewn, with smaller trees sparsely scattered. The walls on either side of Limbo were a constant reminder to Mortuus that Hell was eternally present on the other side of the facade.

Now the terrain flattened as they approached Graz, the next populated village. Mortuus and Darius peeked inside the doorways of several cottages and saw people talking around fireplaces and tables, others with books spread out, and still others who stared at the quartet warily. The doorways were carved with flowering vines, flowers, fruits, animals or geometric shapes. The village had a cobblestone path winding through it. Darius noticed the cobblestones were engraved, just like the doorways, in an ornate fashion.

"Barak?" asked Darius. "Why do the people of this village engrave their road stones?" Barak looked at the stones, considering the many shapes and wordings.

"In this village, many artists and art appreciators congregate. They desire to make everything around them beauteous," answered Barak.

"Even the cobblestones? I understand the woodwork on the doorways, but isn't it a bit tedious to shape and craft every stone?"

Barak chided, "Well, if you would be logical, there is little need here for a cobblestone path, Darius. The people did not have to bother themselves, but they created this path anyway. Though it seems overly decorative, we do have a lot of time when eternity is the measure."

Darius nodded in good humor to his companions' grins.

"Of course, of course," he muttered with a shy grin. "I knew that. Perhaps I will also have too much time to spend here, and I too will become an artisan road stone carver. This is what I wish for."

The carved stone path took them out to the other side of Graz in short order, where they continued walking through more rocky terrain, and two smaller villages; the first, Almere, on their left, and the second village, Rennes, on the right. Socius and Barak began talking just past Rennes.

"Barak, what was Benjamin talking about when he said we have been complacent?" inquired Socius. Barak was hesitant to answer, trying to decide what he should share with Socius, and what he should hold back. He was uncomfortable keeping the information from his friend, but there were some controversies that were too dangerous to share with anyone. Still, it was Benjamin that had opened this Pandora's Box, and Socius was a trustworthy friend. The events which had recently unfolded could only mean the change that had been foretold since the earliest days was in progress. They would consult Clavius to confirm this fact.

"I will tell you, Socius. I will tell you all just as soon as we see Clavius. For now, I will not alarm you and our guests needlessly. I ask for your patience until we visit Clavius." Socius, Mortuus and Darius were more curious than ever. "I promise to give you full disclosure *when* we get confirmation. Please save the questions which I see already on your faces." The three men, staring at Barak, were silent, stifling their many questions.

They soon approached very large piles of stone and small boulders, stacked directly in front of the path. Barak led them to the left, where it appeared the stone piles went all the way to the wall on the Acheron-side of Limbo. The path directly narrowed so that only a single person could pass through at a time, squeezing between smaller rock piles that had been assembled purposely to alter the trail.

Almost at the wall, an opening appeared on the right, and the men followed it to a giant excavated pit, rounded, with ledges of concentric circling paths. There was a slope from each ledge down into the ledge below it. A tiny building stood at the bottom center, and there were entryways into two tunnels visible from the location of the four. The rock piles were scattered all around the crater, blocking an easy trek through this area. A ledge went around from their edge on the right side, all the way around to a small opening that was the continuation of the path they were on. Moving toward the edge of the pit, Mortuus looked down to see that they were quite far from the bottom. It was perhaps the most uninviting scenery he had beheld since entering Limbo; a picture of man-made devastation that seemed a blight to even the barren rocky landscape. He hoped the area beyond the pit would return to the well-treed, grassy forest floor that he had come to love in his short time in Limbo.

"You see the ledge around the pit?" said Barak, addressing Mortuus and Darius. "We'll take it to the other side. This, by the way, is where we mine metals. This pit was created long ago, when the walls were constructed, and only now is it providing us with a good amount of metal ore. The ores are refined in the building at the bottom – it's bigger than it appears from our vantage point, and –"

"Barak, Socius, look! Demons!" warned Mortuus in a loud whisper. Barak moved closer, holding his hands up to signal Mortuus to silence.

Far across the giant pit, two large flyer demons had suddenly appeared from behind a large rock pile, and looked as if they were flying straight for the men. As soon as they neared the center of the pit, they dove, circling downward until they at last pulled their wings in and landed roughly, near one of the mine entrances. Mortuus and Darius looked at Barak, surprised to see him appear undisturbed by the menacing presence of the creatures.

"We will wait until they finish their business and leave the mine. It will not be long. Let's have a seat back behind the piles, where we came in." said Barak pointing backward toward the path between the piles. The men walked until they were hidden within the pit entrance, though Barak sat just near enough to see into the open area.

"For your information, those demons work in the smith shop adjoining the whirlpool building, which we are going to avoid. They come to the pit to take a share of the refined metals." said Barak.

"What do the demons do with metal?" asked Darius.

"The demons have a forge in their smithy shop. Some of our better blacksmiths have dared to venture inside to see what kind of instruments they create, but they were quickly chased away. It's said that they use magic to forge their weapons. I would surmise that is mainly because they have no skills of their own." said Barak. "As for the use, I expect their hooks and other crude torture devices are created from the ore."

"Who is required to mine the ore?" asked Mortuus.

"No one is *required* to mine" said Barak. "Believe it or not, our chief miner, Eruo, and his fellows actually enjoy the digging. Some folks like to get their hands dirty once in a while."

"He enjoys mining? Isn't that dangerous? Do they have cave-ins, or get trapped?" asked Darius. "I don't see the point of it." Darius had developed his own subservient philosophy of survival that he hadn't shaken in all his years on earth and in the Vestibule. It was along the lines of, don't do anything you aren't told to and find the quickest, most efficient way of getting through each task because there is no art or enjoyment to it. All toil, in Darius' mind, was duty, effort, burden, grind.

"Eruo has had a few troubles in the mines, but after many centuries, he's pretty well got it down. Some folks like the dig, some do it for the common good, others for a change of scenery. Limbo will get boring after you've been here a few years." Barak smiled and winked at Mortuus, forgetting the angst of Socius momentarily, "Lucky for you both that Aristotle felt the same way."

Seeing Socius' grim face, Barak corrected himself with a cough of embarrassment and looked out over the pit, motioning the others to come silently behind him.

"Look there my friends. The creatures carry a load of refined iron in their sacks."

The three men gathered around behind Barak, and saw far away, the creatures, each heavily burdened with a large sack, bigger than their bodies. The sacks appeared too large to be carried by the winged demons, yet, one by one, they flew upward with relative ease.

"Magic." said Barak abruptly. "We believe they have temporarily removed the mass from the iron. The magic will wear off after they return to the smithy."

"Amazing!" said Darius.

"How do you know of this magic, Barak?" asked Socius.

"Long ago, the Great Library contained many books on Fallen magic." said Barak. "No one could read or understand the tomes. In fact, the books were quite large and heavy, so rare few even attempted to borrow them. Then, one day, mysteriously, the tomes disappeared. No one ever learned how or why."

"Why could no one read the books, Barak?" asked Mortuus.

"They were written in the language of the Angelics." replied Barak. "None except for the Fallen can understand."

"Angelics?" asked Mortuus, his interest piqued.

"They are more commonly referred to as Angels," answered Barak. "The Chronicler believes Aristotle found the missing tomes just before awakening you, Mortuus." Socius became excited.

"The tomes in the room before the Hallway!" he cried, "Of course! But why hide them if no one can interpret the language?"

"Because someone deciphered the language." said Darius. "Or the Fallen believed someone had. Or could."

"Very good, Darius." said Barak. "Fallen magic can be very powerful. In the wrong hands, it could be used against the Fallen. We believe they came to understand this, and hid the books in their secret undertomb area. Another reason for their anger with Aristotle."

"So you have read the latest logs of Aristotle." said Socius. "How did you find out th-" Barak, still watching the flying demons, interrupted Socius.

"In good time, Socius." replied Barak. "We must get past the pit before the beasts return."

The group crossed the pit via the narrow ledge around the top. The rocks were small and bothered the feet of those who were barefooted, namely Mortuus and Darius, but they did not complain. Barak kept a quick pace, constantly scanning ahead for demons. When they had almost reached the far side, two men, miners, shouted up from the bottom of the pit, waving at the group to wait. The miners climbed fast, using handholds to scale the walls straight up to the ledge where the four men stood.

"Hail thee Barak! What news have you?" asked one of the miners. Barak nodded his head, chuckling. Abreo, a short, plump, round-faced man, dirty from the mine dust, approached like a pre-pubescent boy, innocent and friendly, smiling white teeth emphasizing the dirt on his face. Barak was reminded of a dog he had loved in his life, which would wag its tail furiously at the sight of any newcomer. Behind Abreo, a taller, more serious looking miner, also covered in the dust, walked toward the group, eyeballing Darius and Mortuus suspiciously. He was a grim sort, and contrasted sharply with his fellow miner in gaunt appearance and behavior toward the transiting group. He had immediately altered his gait upon sighting the garb of Mortuus and Darius. It made the pair of newcomers to Limbo self-conscious.

"Hello Abreo, Exaro." said Barak. "We need to pass through before the demons return. May I speak with you of your news later? We must avoid the flyers." said Barak.

"They will not return for some time, Barak. They have cleaned out all of our stockpiles. At least they believe they have." said Abreo, smiling mischievously and winking.

"Well, good news then. What other news have you, Abreo? I know you well enough to see it is you who have information to share. You may go first; I know I can hardly get a word in when you have something on your mind. Speak to us Abreo."

Abreo was looking at the other three men, particularly Mortuus.

"Oh yes, introductions first. Abreo, Exaro, these are our friends Darius and Mortuus, and you know-"

"Socius! It has been forever! Look how you have grown! He is getting big, isn't he Exaro? I think it's been almost a century since – " The chubby miner was cut off by his associate.

"Far longer, Abreo." Exaro teased. "Why do you wait so long my friend? I know you do not like the underground, or the company we keep..."

Barak whispered a clarification to Darius and Mortuus. "He means the demons."

"...But we'll come out for you if you visit once in a while." Exaro looked at Mortuus and Darius, studying them again.

"Newcomers?" Exaro prodded as he examined them toe to head, stopping and staring abruptly at Darius. "Why do you wear the robes of outer Hell? I..."

"Exaro, mind your business." quipped Abreo, seeing the discomfort on the faces of the four men. The mood changed to uncertainty, and Abreo was doing what he could to remedy it. He was also curious about these men, but his desire to know did not supersede his desire for good manners. And he wanted badly to share his news, above all.

"I'm sorry - we cannot stay and talk my friends." said Socius. Barak was looking at him and nodding. Socius did not want Mortuus and Darius put off by these old acquaintances, nor did Socius want any information about the fact that they were not proper inhabitants of

Limbo known outside of a few people. "We have to move on - we have business past Basel."

"Wait my friends." pleaded Abreo. "Please excuse Exaro's...abruptness. I have news that I would discuss with you. It will not take long. Then you can continue on your journey. But please stay, just a bit longer."

"I am afraid of your demon guests returning, Abreo. Really, we should be going," said Barak, "But I promise to return and visit for as long as you like, later." Barak was using this as an excuse to get away before the unwanted questioning continued. Mortuus and Darius stood, not knowing how to act in this uncomfortable situation. "I give you my word-"

"Hear me out, Barak, Socius. Believe me, there will be no demons, not for a long time. They took a great share of our latest work just before you arrived. Your friends are welcome, by all means." Abreo turned to Exaro, and shot him a glance, indicating he should affirm Abreo's assertion.

"Stay, friends. Please. You should hear this." said a more softened and duly chastised Exaro. He looked pleadingly at the four.

Socius nodded at Barak, who reluctantly agreed. All six men sat on the ground. Smiling and anxious, Abreo told his news like an anxious gossip. His manner was solemn, but his countenance could not portray such seriousness, like a small child who describes an event with importance far beyond his years. It was an endearing quality of Abreo's, and he had no clue whatsoever it existed.

"Many centuries ago, as you know, we began mining f-". Exaro cut him off sharply.

"To the point already, Abreo. Barak can listen to the Chronicler if he needs the entire history of Limbo." He was a no nonsense sort, and he knew his friend would recite the history of mining in Limbo from the beginning of time if he was left to his own devices. Abreo gave a mock salty look in his naturally humorous way, then restarted.

"We speak with the demons on occasion to find out what they know or what they may be up to. On this last visit, they were quite anxious to take as much iron as we had, not that they usually leave us much anyway. Did any of you notice the size of the load they carried?"

The four nodded. "It was quite large," answered Barak.

Abreo continued, "They are in chaos. It seems that they have a secret area in the tombs. That's the Seventh Circle, by the way."

"Sixth," corrected Socius.

"Right. The Sixth Circle," said Abreo. "They have an underground where they keep prisoners isolated and unconscious. This area is unknown to most of the demons, and is visited by Fallen regularly."

"How do you know of this?" asked Socius.

"Eruo," replied Exaro, "He speaks with them." Abreo nodded in agreement as the four men appeared to be in shock. Abreo spoke again. "On this visit, they were angry, speaking of the 'wrath of the masters' that came upon their fellows who work in that secret underground. One captive escaped, and they only very recently found out about it. The Fallen were so angry, they destroyed their own workers. Probably through some sort of magic I suppose. They relocated several workers from the whirlpool building to replace them. To top it off, they have upped the expected quotas of weaponry from the pool house smithies."

"Demons," whispered Barak to Mortuus and Darius.

"Yes, worker demons. And that is why I was so certain they would not return while we spoke, Barak. They have more than enough metals and far fewer hands to forge their weapons. That last pair was as bedraggled looking as I've ever seen them." Abreo took a deep breath as his story came to an end, "...And that is all I needed to tell you."

Looking around at his guests, Abreo proceeded carefully, "I must say, you ventured past our pit at quite an interesting time." He spoke slowly and deliberately, "I will not question it, and nor will Exaro," Abreo said, nodding in Exaro's direction, "I will only say I am quite curious... and... I would like to hear your new friends' stories sometime." Abreo was running out of hints, but his curiosity was overwhelming, "Pity you must be going. This giant one looks to have quite a good story. I have never seen such robes either. I don't believe any of the weavers in Porto carry such fine threads."

Mortuus and Darius glanced at each other, waiting for either Barak or Socius to make a move. These were their friends, after all.

"And now you are being rude, Abreo." said Exaro. "We must let our friends continue their trek, though I, admittedly, am also curious. I will not, however, hold you to remain longer if you desire to leave. We do enjoy the company, and Abreo was getting unbearable and really needed to share the news."

"And it is good you have shared this news, Abreo. Barak, I think we need to trust our friends." said Socius finally. "May I share our news?"

"Very well" said Barak after a few moments.

Socius began recounting the story of the newly arrived pair, and everything he knew since Aristotle awakened Mortuus. Very early on in the telling, Abreo and Exaro were both pleased that they had persuaded the group to stay.

It was a long tale, uninterrupted by flying demons.

Chapter 40
Clavius' Secret

Abreo and Exaro were beside themselves. After listening to Socius, and confirming his recollection of events with Mortuus and Darius, the two miners quizzed the pair intensely. Abreo asked Darius about the gate, as he had a longstanding belief that if any newcomer had just turned around he might be able to go back out the way he came. Exaro scoffed as Darius told of his attempts to exit. Both miners were in complete disbelief at the story of Charon's drowning until hearing Socius eyewitness account of seeing the empty skiff. Abreo got excited over the incident of Mortuus and the demon Morpheus, clapping his hands in a victorious display.

"He does not much like demons." said Exaro as he pointed at Abreo. "One of them kicked him around when it thought he was hiding extra supplies."

"Of course, I *was*." replied Abreo. "But we always do. This one just decided to have a problem about it. I felt like I had been trampled by a herd of bulls. It broke most of my ribs. I didn't think I'd ever regenerate again, but you killed it by strangulation? Impossible! They are too strong! And, how did you hang onto the beast for so long? Shouldn't he have ripped you apart long before it expired? What did –" Abreo was nearly rabid in his excitement, firing questions at Mortuus fast and furiously. It took the better part of several hours before the four men were able to get on their feet to resume their journey. When they were finally on the way, Barak made a last inquiry of the road ahead.

"Abreo, is there any trouble likely when we pass the whirlpool building? Anything we need concern ourselves with?"

"Nothing I am aware of." said Abreo. "There should be fewer flyers since they lost a portion of their staff, but they may have Fallen visiting. Send someone ahead or take the far path." He stopped for a moment, twitching his nose almost imperceptibly, like a tiny mouse. "You may want a change of garb for Darius also; he's very noticeable in that death shroud, and Mortuus, your robes could use replacing. They are clean but raggedy for Limbo and there's no place between here and the whirlpool to re-clothe either of you."

Darius and Mortuus were nonplussed. They had heard this warning about their clothes many times, feeling more and more vulnerable each time someone pointed it out. Abreo didn't take notice of their discomfort and continued, unabated, and pleased with his solution to the problem, "You will all have to keep your eyes open. Once you reach Porto, you'll find more than a few weavers. And, in Porto, they enjoy dressing newcomers in their fancy clothes."

Exaro chimed in, "And Abreo should know this since he wears the fancy garments himself when we are not at work in the mines. You four must stay to the path against the inside wall when you pass the whirlpool building. The demon's smithy is located on the Acheron side of the pool. Do not forget they can fly! Look upward…often! But never fear, chances are, they will not expect to find their fugitive right under their noses."

"Or you can just destroy them, demon slayer." laughed Abreo.

"Wait until I tell Eruo!" exclaimed Abreo. "Maybe we will strangle one ourselves!" He smiled and winked at Socius. "Goodbye my friends. Thank you for the wonderful news. Stop back on your return if you like. I will provide a wonderful tour of the mines should any of you be interested. You will not believe what we have been doing down there these last few centuries."

With a wave, the four turned and resumed their trip. The two miners stood watching as they departed, then returned to their mining.

The four followed the twisted path around various rock piles on the far side of the pit until the way at last became straight and open and led out to rocky, flat terrain similar to the path they had taken to the pit. Here, they had the advantage of being able to spot anything approaching for a long distance and they were relieved to know, via Abreo and Exaro, the demons would not be passing overhead for some time. Mortuus saw green in the distance. The group was near to the wall on the right. For one moment, Mortuus thought he could hear a loud wind.

After a long walk, the four men arrived at the edge of a stand of trees, and soon were surrounded by full forest. Short green grass, bordered with taller grasses highlighted the way, and the smell of the forest's freshness permeated the air. Mortuus imagined he could remain here for eternity very easily. At the same time, he brooded over Benjamin's talk of escape. It was far better here than outer Hell. Why would Aristotle even have wanted to venture outside? Why would anyone want to escape Limbo for the outside?

More questions surged within the thoughts of Mortuus. What had he done to deserve his specific punishment? Why had he been placed in an 'eternal sleep'? What memories had he lost; why would they be wiping his memories? And, why would they want to hide him and the others, as Socius and Barak suspected? Others? Like Mortuus? Surveying the landscape, Mortuus decided he would not trouble himself over these questions he could not answer. For now, the trees, the grass, and the other scents of Limbo were all he needed. Answers could wait until he had his fill of this place.

The whirlpool building was visible in the distance. It was longer than the Hall of Science was high. The group emerged from the wooded path to see a large reservoir, a giant bubbling lake tightly lined with trees. Sparsely jutting out from shore were rocky ledges. The pool was so large it seemed that it would be impossible to swim across, though unlike Acheron and the Styx, no mist shrouded the far edge. The four men went to the nearest opening in the trees, keeping constant watch for flying demons that might be traveling overhead.

"My friends, welcome to the Second Waters. Please help yourselves," said Barak. Mortuus was not thirsty, but the sparkling water did entice. He and Darius drank a small handful. One taste and the pair began drinking ravenously. This water had a strange effect. The pair finished and stood up in some confusion, not understanding what why they felt disoriented.

"Did you enjoy your drink? This is a cleansing water." said Socius. "The First Waters are generally considered potent for regenerating. Drinking of the Second Waters seems to enhance the effect of the first. Many newcomers feel lightly intoxicated. This will wear off, and after you will feel more at ease within yourself. It is believed this water diminishes the stress of a person's lifetime, though there is no discernible proof. I was an infant when I arrived in Limbo, so I cannot say for certain."

"You see the building on the far end of this lake?" asked Barak of Mortuus and Darius, "That is built across the top of the whirlpool."

"Why would they erect a building over the whirlpool?" asked Mortuus.

"I am curious about that also." added Darius.

"These waters feed the whirlpool." said Socius. "Do you know of the concept of reincarnation?" Darius and Mortuus both shook their heads. Socius continued. "When infants die they are immediately brought to the whirlpool. We call it the Whirlpool of Reincarnation. The infants are placed into a basket, and are floated into the whirlpool. According to the legend, the children return to Earth, reborn into a new life. It is a great point of interest in Limbo, but we know no more than what I tell you. Many here would gladly throw themselves into the whirlpool, but only infants are permitted since they have been unfairly taken from life." Mortuus and Darius listened with fascination.

"They return to another life? You mean they escape Hell? How do the infants get into Hell? Why would children be brought here at all? Who walks them to the gate of Limbo?" queried Darius, disquieted at the thought of such innocence being subjected to Hell.

"We are not certain how they get through Hell, nor why they are even brought. The Elders tell us they simply appear within the Keep. They are charged with bringing the infants to the whirlpool. The workers allow only Elders inside the building, but they are not permitted to wander. The building is guarded by Fallen magic, and only Fallen and certain demon workers may enter. Many people have tried; most have been dissuaded by the demons and magical traps."

"Have any succeeded?" asked Mortuus.

"We do not know. None have returned who have attempted. For all we know, they may be stuck under the water forever, or have been carried to outer Hell."

"But they push a baby into a whirlpool, regardless? Without knowing for sure? That is too horrific!" Darius was visibly outraged, surprising Mortuus, who had come to know him as a basically steady fellow, unassuming and almost stoic. This was more emotion than Mortuus had seen from him since they met. "As for grown people to make the attempt, I understand. It makes sense," Darius continued, "I might try, but only after I tired of Limbo." And, with that he folded his arms across his chest, frowning.

"How many attempted before the Fallen decided to build a structure over it and heavily guard it?" Mortuus asked in a calming tone.

"Roughly five are commonly known about, Mortuus," answered Barak, "And that is confirmed by the Chronicler, so I expect it is accurate. Many believe that we would return to a new life, start over again, while others believe that we would be rejected by the reincarnating magic and transported to the lower circles. Limbo is not so bad, as you have seen, but after many centuries it may become tiresomely predictable. Those five who attempted to escape did so when Limbo was still dark and barren, and no walls yet existed. There was no direct torment, but the sounds and smells of outer Hell permeated our being, and the eternal darkness weighed on us, making our mood always gloomy. Now we keep ourselves busy with arts, education, games, hobbies, crafts, and storytelling. All citizens are aware of their great fortune. Rare few exit the gate you fought so hard to enter."

"How do people enter Limbo?" asked Mortuus. "I saw no one at the gate when I passed. And I waited there for a long time when I first climbed to this circle."

"Everyone who is a proper citizen of Limbo enters through the mirror of Minos. When the people enter for judgment, they are required to look at their reflection; in fact, once they enter the room where the mirror is located, they are naturally compelled toward the mirror. Then the individual is transported to their eternal placement, be it here or in outer Hell. I know you do not remember, Mortuus, but Darius, you must recall that fateful trip. Can you tell us what you experienced? I myself stared into the silver glass, dreading what I would see. The image in the mirror looked back; it was me, but it smiled...and then I was standing next to the Keep. I sat there until a guard came over and asked if I was okay. I said I did not know where I was, and so he explained, understanding I was a newcomer. I cannot tell you how relieved I was."

Darius winced at Barak's story. His encounter with the mirror was an entirely different experience, and part of his torment had been remembering it as he was chased and stung by the Hell Flies. Darius swallowed, a little reluctant to tell his story, but also drawn toward it as if it were a confession he needed to make.

"My version is very bad, Barak. You remember I was sentenced to the Vestibule. I saw my entire life, in but a moment, and the pain I had caused upon others. Each second I felt all of the transgressions I committed upon others, as if each was being inflicted on me. I experienced everything firsthand; I was each person whom I harmed." Darius stopped speaking, an expression of pain on his face. "The recollection makes me cringe."

He looked quickly into the eyes of his companions. He was not that eager to reveal his shame, but when his gaze met that of Mortuus, Darius was calmed and his reluctance subsided.

"You see, I was a slave," he went on, "My people were conquered, and the survivors were enslaved just before my birth. I was raised as the property of a wealthy aristocrat, and imbued with the values of a proper servant. I endured much abuse, never complaining and always eager to give more. I became the best slave, my master's favorite, and I played this role to the point of informing on my fellows. It was as any virtuous slave would do. Those who I turned in, who only wished to escape from their lives of captivity and daily abuse, would, at worst, be put to death and in the least, be beaten severely."

He took a quick glance around and, seeing no look of judgment on any of his companion's faces, but rather, interest, and maybe even empathy, Darius went on, "My life wasn't much better for my 'virtue.' I still toiled and slaved like everyone else, I was still beaten on the whim of my master or his wife and children, but I was relatively safer from scrutiny, which allowed me brief moments of sanctuary. And I could occasionally expect table scraps and cleaner clothes since I was required to be in their presence more than the others."

Darius was now looking down at his bare feet; his toe had dug a tiny indent into the gravelly loam, "My guilt, which I attempted to banish from memory, weighed heavily on me by the vision's end. I loathed the person who stood before me. I thought it odd that my image was sobbing, loudly, though I was not. A moment later, I stood in the Vestibule, and was collected into a herd by the vicious insects." Mortuus and the others looked at Darius's saddened face, seeing clearly he was still haunted by his experience.

"We shall add your story to the collection of the Chronicler, Darius. His students study every individual's personal entrance into Hell and Limbo. Up until now we have only information on how we enter Limbo," said Barak. "The students will greatly value your personal story. We will endeavor to keep your identity a secret, however. The Elders Council and their followers are not so open to your presence."

Socius interrupted. "How many students does the Chronicler have, Barak?"

"We do not keep count. Some attend at the behest of the Elders. Others do not attend consistently. A rough guess would be about one hundred." Barak paused, freezing in motion. As the group watched, a lone man came jogging down the path. The man, seeing the group, waved hello as he passed by and continued down the path. Barak had a sudden look of concern on his face. Socius saw this, and studied the runner, who was moving away from the group.

"It is time to go." said Barak. "That runner was sent to alert others whom the Chronicler trusts that something is happening. He has been newly assigned, and was stationed by the Keep. We shall follow the path away from the whirlpool building as Abreo suggested. We arrive in Terni next."

The group of four continued their walk. Darius and Mortuus nervously watched the building, slightly on their left. The path split off to the right, veering away from the building and toward the inner wall. The largess of the building disappeared as the path became tightly clad within dense tree growth, though occasionally it became visible through small gaps.

At length, the men noticed the building passed into the distance behind them. They walked by individuals and small groups of people sitting in patches of grass on their left as Barak and Socius scanned overhead for flyers, just to be sure. Mortuus saw why they decided to take this path; there was only a sliver of visibility overhead due to the thick forest canopy. They journeyed uneventfully until they reached a tiny village that appeared out of a clearing. There were only two dozen buildings, all built off of each other. A winding path of plain cobblestone trailed through and led to more thick forest on the other side of the buildings. Another path merged smoothly near the center of the village.

"Welcome to Terni." said Barak. "If you like wood and jewelry crafts, this is the place you visit."

Wooden tables lay at the center of the village, spread out. Inhabitants of the area sat around these tables. One group was carving ornate shapes out of chunks of wood. Another was crafting small jewelry items, which Barak told Mortuus and Darius were all from the metal mine. One short man, of thin frame and somewhat skeletal appearance, was pounding glowing iron with a small hammer against a small anvil, heating the small sliver over a red hot forge, and then pounding it, repeating the cycle many times. The glow and heat of the forge reminded Mortuus of the burning tombs in the Sixth Circle. Small, multicolored stones sat in a large bowl on a wooden table next to the thin man's forge and anvil. The man looked up for a moment, studying the visitors faces, then returned nonchalantly back to his work.

"Barak – what are those small stones used for?" said Mortuus as he pointed toward the wooden table. Barak looked over at the table, examining the tiny, colorful stones.

"They are for decorating the jewelry." said Barak. "Those stones are a byproduct of the mining that Eruos, Abreo and Exaro do. That man probably extracts the stones, or has another do it, from the large piles of rocks all around the mining pit."

"I see." said Mortuus. "I will bet he makes very nice jewelry with those. They remind me of a larger stone I found for Phlegyas."

"Phlegyas?" replied Socius. "I do not recall you speaking of the oarsman, at least not regarding any stone."

"I did not have the time earlier to speak of Phlegyas."

"I am interested to hear," said Socius. "Did Phlegyas require you to do something for him? I recall Aristotle having to perform a dangerous quest for Phlegyas before the oarsman would transport him to the far shore. It must be his test as to whether he will trust you."

"I had to find a tomb," said Mortuus. "It had special markings and hid a carved stone skull underneath. It opened by use of magic incantation. Phlegyas taught me the spell, and had me repeat it many times so I would not forget. The spell made me feel weak. The skull lay in a place of that circle -"

"The Sixth Circle." said Barak.

"Yes, the Sixth Circle. The area was swarming with imps." said Mortuus. "I almost failed the quest. I was savagely attacked by one and sure that I would be found by the whole host of the others. Thankfully, a small building nearby served to conceal me as I slay the small beasts, one at a time. I remained until I had regenerated enough to continue my search."

"Phlegyas sent you into a pack of imps!?!" exclaimed Socius. "Aristotle told me that his quest was similarly dangerous; Phlegyas eventually accepted the vials of water for passage. After many years, Phlegyas required only news from Aristotle's travels. The oarsman especially liked to hear of the Master Centaur, Chiron."

"That must be why Phlegyas had a small supply on hand. He gave me a few vials when I returned with the skull."

"Of what use was the stone skull to the oarsman?" asked Darius. "Was it beautiful, or –"

"I would guess it had magical properties." said Barak. "The Chronicler has spoken of magical objects on very few occasions. They are believed to be hidden in outer Hell by the Fallen and are quite rare."

"Why do the Fallen not keep the items at their homesteads, wherever it is they reside? Where do Fallen reside?" asked Mortuus.

"No one knows," replied Barak. "They are very rarely seen, and only fly upward through the mist. Aristotle witnessed them on a few occasions; the centaurs have had encounters with Fallen also, though long ago. Our closest contact is with Azza's imp. Azza is the name of one of the Fallen. His imp only passes messages to the Elders Council."

"What did the skull look like, Mortuus?" asked Darius. "Did you notice anything strange about it?"

"The skull was a container for another item. I discovered it as I sat waiting for Phlegyas. I did not want him to know I had opened the skull. Phlegyas did not speak of it, and at that time I did not care for anything except to get to Limbo."

"What was in the skull?" asked Barak.

"A large gem, about the size of a hundred of those small stones," said Mortuus. "It was clear and beautiful, like the First Waters. The feeling I got when I touched it was strange. I felt that I had to protect it, to save it from this place. Have any of you ever felt such a thing?"

"No," said Barak, "But your reaction is intriguing."

"I have many questions for the Chronicler, Barak," said Mortuus.

"You will get answers in time," Barak assured Mortuus, "We need to increase our pace. I had forgotten that a few close friends and supporters of the Elders Council reside in this village. Let's hurry to Porto and get you two proper clothing. Clavius awaits."

"Who is Clavius, Barak?" asked Darius, whose demeanor had become lighter since his drink at the Second Waters and the subsequent telling of his life experiences.

"Clavius? Well, he is a scientist-miner-loner, Darius. Clavius was once one of the senior scientists, on the lines of Benjamin; then he just up and resigned suddenly, no one knows why. After, he went to work in the mines with Abreo, Exaro and Eruo. He was there for many years, but would provoke the demons often. At first he attempted to converse with the beasts. They were not friendly to his questioning, and so he backed off. Later, he was caught eavesdropping on their conversations. They beat him severely on more than one occasion for that transgression. Eventually he quit working in the mines too. Abreo said he was a natural at mining and that they were sad to lose him."

"Hmm. What a strange thing to do, talking to demons," thought Mortuus out loud, "Why are we going to meet Clavius again?"

"Clavius has accumulated a certain specialized skill," Barak answered simply, "But we are almost there, my friends. You will see what I mean soon enough."

They passed into the wooded area and reached the small village of Porto in the same amount of time it took for them to get from their whirlpool stop to Terni. Barak, increasingly concerned, and angry with himself for forgetting about the Elder's friends in Terni, urged the four to move quickly.

"This is Porto. We will find Clavius so that Mortuus' origin can be confirmed. Socius, you will find proper clothing for Mortuus and Darius. There are many weavers and tailors here. If you can, find a larger pack for each as well." Socius nodded and disappeared between two cottages. Barak motioned the pair to follow. They walked through the grouping of cottages until they reached a small, unkempt homestead, unoriginal in appearance. It seemed plain, not noticeable.

Barak knocked three times in a rhythmic order. Immediately after the third knock, the door opened, and out stepped a small, squatty man, looking as if a giant had been compressed down to a fifth of its size; the wide square frame and head a caricature of a full grown adult. The strangely built man looked at Barak, then eyeballed Darius and Mortuus, scrutinizing each from head to toe. He gestured the men to come in hurriedly. The windows were shuttered closed; the darkness was unsettling for all three visitors.

"Do not speak until we are in, my friends," whispered the compacted man in a deep, gruff voice. Mortuus and Darius were puzzled, but knew there was always more than meets the eye in Limbo. A clicking noise crossed the cottage, followed by a grinding sound, emanating from underneath the three. Mortuus was reminded of the Sixth Circle and the tomb with the skull hidden under it. Suddenly, an opening appeared in the darkness, and a stairwell was revealed which went down into a well lit hallway. "This way, please, hurry," said the square man.

The three men, followed by the dwarfish man, climbed down the steps. The stairs were steep and narrow, and each man stretched out his hands to hold himself upright between the side walls all the way down.

"You should consider installing a handrail for people to hold onto, Clavius," said Barak. Clavius did not answer. He was intent on getting the three inside. The descent was far deeper than it initially appeared. They heard the grinding noise again, though it was louder, and over their heads, and they knew the passage was closed.

"Darius, Mortuus, I would like to introduce you to Clavius. Clavius, this is Mortuus an-" Barak was cut off.

"Keep walking Barak. Introductions come later," ordered Clavius. The hallway at the bottom of the steps continued far out of sight, lit with an unseen source of light from the ceiling. Mortuus was growing anxious as he was reminded of the undertomb he had escaped after his awakening. The hallway was carved out of solid stone, with rough walls that had no doors or indication of any openings, but soon, after only a minute's walk in the seemingly endless tunnel, Clavius stopped. Turning toward an indistinguishable section of wall to the right, Clavius abruptly, and very loudly, cleared his throat.

"*Ostendo!*" trumpeted Clavius at the plain rock wall. With a low rumble, a crack appeared in the wall, then an outline appeared in the shape of a semicircle. The piece of wall pulled away from Clavius, forming a deep depression.

"Amazing!" Darius murmured as he bent his head to look at the new opening. The rock piece that pulled back was sliding to the right, disappearing from view behind the wall. The opening was large enough for all to enter at once. The inside entryway opened to a giant cavern, complete with stalactites and stalagmites, crystalline and icy in appearance. A small path went down a slope to the cavern floor. The path was twisted and hidden partially by the columns of stalactites hanging down and meeting the stalagmites, as if the cave was a giant fanged vampiric mouth. A rectangle of bright light marked an opening at the end of the path.

"Clavius, how did you find this place?" asked Mortuus.

"My friend, when you have centuries, you get a lot of work done. I used to toil with Abreo and Eruo at the pit. Once I learned the spells the demons used for excavating rock, I used it repeatedly to create this long hallway. The Fallen have no idea that a human can perform their magic. Having a lot of strengthening and rejuvenating potions helps too," smiled Clavius.

"Where does the hallway end? I would like to see how far it goes."

"The hallway length is an illusion. The tunnel ends not so far away as it appears, though the lighting creates the illusion of great distance. There are traps set to capture anything that tries to go all the way to the end, so if Fallen or demons get in here, they will not find us too easily. Weapons are also hidden inside the walls."

"Amazing," repeated Darius. "What is that light at the end of the path? Is that where we are headed?"

"Yes. That is my laboratory," replied Clavius. The group followed Clavius down the slope and across the floor of the giant cave.

"Do you need to close the entry way?" offered Barak.

"Socius can do it when he gets here. I am tired. The magic has taken much of my strength. Next time I'll use the wall lever instead of showing off," smiled Clavius, a little weary looking. "Gods, I am exhausted."

Mortuus and Darius, their interests greatly aroused, examined every step of the path, and the whole cavern. The stalactites shimmered where the light from the opening struck them, sparkling like miniscule diamonds. The crystalline outside made it look as if snow had fallen. The two newcomers stopped for short intervals of sightseeing, but were hastened along by Barak and Clavius if they slowed. Soon they had crossed the canyon floor and were at the steps to a large, well lit, doorway. Mortuus grew nervous, more anxious because of what Benjamin had said. Soon he would have knowledge of himself and his origin.

He was as frightened as he was excited.

Chapter 41
Panos on the Rill

Panos made it to the rill. It was a difficult climb up the side with his mangled, baked body, but as he slowly moved his body off the burning plain, he regenerated, and the incredible pain began to diminish. Once Panos was fully off the scorching sand, he lay still. Feeling the pain slowly ebb away, he crawled to the flat top of the rill. A hot, red, coppery smelling stream ran through it. It had eroded a deep furrow into the rock. Panos lay on his back, looking around for the demons that dropped him earlier. He did not know that they were loathe to come down to the fiery plain. He would have been easily picked up if they had the courage to pursue him under fire.

When he had enough energy, the fugitive from the Vestibule sat up. He had lain at the top of the rill, staring upward long enough to ascertain he was not being pursued or watched by any sky creatures. He thought about his friends; the demons still had Aetos and Darius, for all he knew. Panos stood up, letting the blood flow to his regenerating legs. He knew the demons had flown to the lower circles, and so decided he would follow the stream and go toward the source of the flow. His plan would take Panos back and away from where demons take fugitives - the boiling pitch according to Philo. The red stream must be flowing down to the lower circles, he reasoned. Philo had been right; Hell got worse farther from the Vestibule. Panos wanted to go back, to have just one more bath in the pool. He imagined feeling the coolness of the water again. Next time he would be sure to watch out for the flying beasts. He was lonely and saddened about the loss of his companions, and hoped they had a way, like him, to make it back.

Panos had few friends in his life. He had been a traveler, nomadic and adventurous right up to his death in his late twenties. His parents forced him to assist them in their duties as Innkeepers, and he had received many slaps and tweaks to his ears when he was caught plying the customers for their tales and experiences in foreign lands. He had caught the wanderers disease, his father had said, an incurable ailment that would leave him no lands or stable source of income in his later years. Determined to cure his son of this wanderlust, the Innkeeper placed heavy burdens of work and chores on Panos, forcing him to work to distract him from socializing with travelers who were passing through. One day, when Panos had reached an age of young adulthood, a band of traveling merchants staying at his father's inn hired him to assist them on the road. Panos disappeared quietly, leaving his parents only a note as to what he was doing. By the time they found his note, he was on a ship far out to sea.

Panos traveled far and wide, seeing the known world of his time, usually as a deck hand or merchant's assistant. He had few friends, as he did not settle down, and would likely not ever see those he met again. Before his death, at the hands of a small group of simple bandits, he had been considering returning to his parent's inn. Panos' wanderlust was waning, and he longed to return to family and friends. In eternity, they were Aetos and Darius. And now they were gone. Did he dare hope again in the land of hopelessness?

The walk was painful, as Panos was not yet fully regenerated from the burning. After a while he saw what looked like trees, far off in the distance. He was sure the heat of this plain must be creating a mirage; how could there be trees in this miserable oven? He eventually realized this was the Wood that Philo spoke of. Panos hastened his pace, scanning the horizon with each agonizing stride. He reached the tree line, the boundary where the burning sands ended and the dense tree growth began.

There was a distinct line which marked two different soils; one soil was heated causing the air above it to distort, the other was a hard, dark clay. This dirt did not appear able to support plants, yet the trees and brush were growing on it plentifully. Panos had not seen a real tree in many centuries and these were a welcome sight indeed. He scanned the forest, wanting to take in all the pleasantness yet realizing there was something odd about the Wood. He cautiously scrutinized the surrounding area. That was when he noticed a movement. He crouched low, and moved back toward the plain, on the rill. The movement stopped, but Panos stayed low.

Then Panos saw it clearly. It was a large beast, not like the demons who took him and his friends. This creature had a beak, like a large bird, but the face seemed very human. It had no arms, only wings at its side and large deadly, talons. It was perched high atop one of the trees, eating leaves. Panos watched as the beast snapped a small branch. The tree made a low moaning sound, as if being tortured. A red liquid flowed from where the branch had broken. The winged creature, disturbed by the noise, decided its meal was over and flew off, oblivious to Panos observing. The fugitive suddenly recalled that Philo called these creatures harpies.

Not wanting an encounter with such a beast, Panos moved further back on the rill, walking slowly, until he was distant enough to feel safe. He noted on his right, a clearing that appeared to pass through the Wood. Panos might have to walk for a short distance on the sands, but he knew he could return to the rill if he got chased by the bird demons. They surely preferred the trees to a burning desert and fireballs.

Panos did too.

Chapter 42
Pholus-At-Large

Pholus reached the forbidden area shortly after Chiron's departure up the rocky slope. He was excited, for he had witnessed his friend and leader of centaur-kind ascend the slope to the Sixth Circle in safety. The Fallen spell of restriction had, for some reason, dissipated. The only remaining concern for Pholus was the half-bull, half-human creature known as the Minotaur; the patroller guardian of the slope and inner perimeter of the Sixth Circle. The beast would rend into pieces any creature that dared get caught.

When the Master Centaur had disappeared from his sight, Pholus trotted toward the forbidden area cave in a relaxed pace. He was enjoying his reclaimed mobility and strength after having regenerated from the mutilation of the harpies. In his mind, Pholus began to entertain the idea of leaving the Seventh Circle. Chiron must be overjoyed, he thought.

The forbidden area was far off, on this side of the river Phlegethon. On the way, Pholus stopped to meet with his commanding officers and their companies. No news, as usual, and even less now that the harpies had been defeated soundly. The herds, however, were happily surprised to see Pholus fully recovered. All had known of his abduction and abuse by the harpies, and more than one of his commanders stated their curiosity at his rapid regeneration.

Chiron's Second in Command noticed many of the companies had busied themselves shooting humans who boiled in the river out of sheer boredom, for sport, and always, for revenge. The silence since the defeat of the harpies had created a great vacuum within the herds, and the many centaurs that had not been able to participate in the battle were restless; eager for any sort of excitement. Humans were the base enemy of all centaurs. No Halfling had ever been unaffected by human brutality and prejudice, and most had met their end at the hands of the marauding hunting parties. Some had been forced to watch their families die, a final act of cruelty that pained them even more than being flayed alive. Pholus, not having shared the experiences of these centaurs, understood their angst, and did not hinder their brutality. The humans were, after all, in their own Hell.

The centaurs had been placed forcibly into this place by the Fallen, and patrolling the Seventh Circle was the duty they had been assigned. Pholus passed a small herd of centaurs, who stopped to bow and salute, then continued on with their targeting game. He would be nearing the forbidden area shortly.

He knew he was near the forbidden area when an imp appeared in the distance. Only within the confines of the forbidden area did the creatures have safe haven in the Seventh Circle. It was here that Nessus stood watch. Nessus, seeing his superior trotting toward him, looked surprised as he bowed to Pholus.

"Report, Nessus," ordered the Second in Command. "What news since last you spoke with Master Chiron?"

"Master Pholus, Sir, there has been little activity to report since I last saw the teacher taken inside the cave."

"Who took the human into the cave? Was it the Fallen, or their workers? asked Pholus.

"Workers sir. There were two flyers, quite large as demons go. The flyers dropped the human, and workers from inside the cave came out and carried the human inside."

"I see," Pholus wanted to storm that cave ever since it had been declared off limits to the herds. This circle was their only place in the afterlife, and an important portion of this circle was denied them, just as humans slowly denied centaur-kind pastures and forest lands during their lives, legislating the herds to live in obscurity. Pholus's mood grew foul.

"Nessus, you will patrol the rocky slopes, where the Minotaur dwells. I want to know when Master Chiron returns, and I want you personally to come and inform me. Do not send an underling, and speak to no one else about this matter. Do you understand?"

"Yes sir," said Nessus. He trotted away slowly, then galloped, and did not look back. Pholus turned to face the cave, watching a pair of imps as they fought with each other. The usual moaning from the Wood across Phlegethon filled the background, punctuated by the occasional shriek and the hollow flapping of the harpies. The foul odors of the burning plains wafted past intermittently. Pholus realized that the tormented of this circle knew about the special area forbidden to centaurs. Special humans were brought to this place for torturing by the demon workers. Pholus grimaced as a new set of screams emanated from the cave mouth.

Abruptly, three of the Fallen flew onto the landing in front of the cave. They looked like semi-giant humans, and as soon as they landed, their massive wings disappeared into their backs. The imps that were fighting at the cave opening scurried away in alarm as the masters of

Hell stormed the entrance. Pholus had only seen the Fallen once before but he was no less awed. It seemed, if Pholus read their body language correctly, that the three were antagonized and agitated. The cave seemed to shake after they entered, and the screaming resumed, unbroken for an extensive period of time. Pholus shuddered, then nearly jumped out of his skin as a hand touched his shoulder.

"By the Dark Gods!" he yelled, throwing his arm up defensively. A small, young centaur, humorously known to the herds as 'Titan' jumped back, away from Pholus.

"Titan, what is it!?!" yelled Pholus. Pholus saw Titan cower. He took a deep breath and softened his words.

"Titan. What do you need? I am very busy now."

"Sir" said the Halfling youth, nervously. "I have news from Master Nessus. The patrols have caught a fugitive."

"A fugitive? Which company?" asked Pholus.

"Commander Equus, sir. He said they caught a human in the midst of the woods, near the clearing. He was being attacked by the harpies. The human had almost gotten through, when they descended on him. The company watched the attack, but decided they must capture the human themselves. They did not clash with the harpies; the avians flew off as soon as Commander Equus and his regiment started toward the flock. The human was shredded badly and fares poorly."

"And so what do they need me to do? They have a strict protocol for these matters. Did they not sound the horn to alert the demons?"

"They said that they would have alerted the demons, but they believe the human is from the upper circles, not the lower. Commander Equus remarked that the human carried the scent of the Vestibule."

"The Vestibule? How did a fugitive get all the way down here? How did he cross the river without us knowing?" Said Pholus.

"He cannot speak yet, Master Pholus. The harpies have damaged his face, mouth and throat quite severely. He will not be able to speak until he has regenerated. Do you have any orders for me to return to Commander Equus or Master Nessus, sir?"

"Detain the prisoner until I arrive. He is not to harm the prisoner. Understood?"

"Yes sir," Titan retreated quickly. Pholus turned back to the cave just in time to see the three Fallen emerge from the cave opening. Their faces were twisted in a spasm of indignation and fury as they walked far enough apart to open their wings. They flew up vertically, with a single flap of their huge wings, vertically, and disappeared into the misty ceiling. Pholus, reputed to be the fiercest of the centaur race, felt veritably insignificant as he witnessed this.

The vermin imps came out of their hiding place and resumed their fight in the front of the cave entrance. Pholus watched, expecting something to happen, and sure enough, the imps abruptly scattered again. Pholus checked the entry way, then looked upward toward the mist, then back at the opening again. The cave darkened a moment before no less than seven demons emerged from the interior, all flyers, each carrying with it iron weapons and metal tools of torture.

"They probably used them on Aristotle. Filthy beasts!" thought Pholus. The flyers spread their wings and ran into the air. They proceeded along and up the incline to the airspace of the Sixth Circle. They were not strong flyers, like the Fallen, but they were all gone a few moments later.

Pholus, hoping his friend's torture session was finished, decided to see to Commander Equus and the human captive. He trotted deliberately toward the shallows of Phlegethon, glancing skyward for Fallen or flyers. He would see to Commander Equus' prisoner from the Vestibule. Surely they must be wrong. If the stranger was from the Vestibule, so far above, how did he get through the river?

Hell was becoming a very chaotic place.

Chapter 43
Old Friends

Chiron could not believe it when he saw his old friend. Reduced to an animalistic state, the sadism of the Fallen was apparent in the twisted appearance of Plutus. Aristotle had described to the Master Centaur the details of Plutus disfiguration, but oral description did not register as deeply as being in the presence of Plutus himself. Studying the rabid, mutated deformity made the pain penetrate into his core. Plutus had been a friend of Chiron's from long before their exile into Hell, and Chiron had hoped to one day meet his old acquaintance again.

Chiron stood near the edge of the Fourth Circle, in the same spot as Mortuus had much earlier. He had had a very difficult time climbing the wall. Centaurs were not built for scaling vertical walls with small footholds. Plutus, catching a scent out of the ordinary coming up the wall, arrived near the ledge just as Chiron clambered over, exhausted and sweating. Chiron stood up to behold his old friend, malformed and twisted, growling. He readied his bow.

Chiron stood his ground and looked into the eyes of this wolf-form of his old friend. They were glazed red, an angry hatred for all that passed through the Fourth Circle. It was the Fallen magic, thought Chiron. He looked deeper, and saw no hope for communicating with Plutus; the friend he knew was buried deeply within the psyche of this beast, unable to take control. The Fallen had imprisoned Plutus within himself.

"My friend" said Chiron, knowing his words were moot, but in hopes of somehow reaching Plutus. "I will return this way to free you from the prison you reside within. If you have any will, permit my passage. You have my word I will do whatever it takes to free you." He stared into the eyes of Plutus, who was edging slowly forward, red eyes glaring. The Master Centaur pulled his bow back, aiming directly at Plutus' chest. "Do not make me release, Plutus."

Plutus knew a bent bow meant pain. Though the bestial creature wanted only to attack, rip, and shred, he moved out of the way of danger. Plutus sidestepped off the rough path between himself and Chiron. He had not so long ago felt the shaft of Aristotle, unbeknownst to Chiron, though his feral mind barely remembered it. Chiron, relieved he would not have to shoot his friend, slightly relaxed. He lowered his bow, and unknowingly provoked the wolf-demon to attack.

Plutus sprang at Chiron, who, in surprise, stumbled backward. Chiron's back legs hung over the cliff. He struggled tenaciously to get back on all four hooves solidly while Plutus was in his face, biting at his throat and clawing any flesh that his deadly claws touched. Chiron became enraged, forcefully shoving Plutus away and regaining his foothold on even ground. Plutus landed on his feet and dug in, jumping at Chiron again. In that short moment, Chiron's legendary archery skills brought down the wolf-beast. With a single arrow going from under his carriage, straight through his right shoulder, and out his back. Plutus stopped a moment to growl and yelp in pain, giving Chiron the opportunity to ready another arrow. Plutus was struck down by the force of the arrow shaft, which stuck out from his belly. He ceased his attack, as the acid from his stomach began leeching into his other internal organs. Plutus lay where he landed, crying in pain. The injury would cause him great discomfort for the remainder of his curse.

Chiron touched his own throat and face, feeling the burning pain of the lacerations. Blood was pumping out of his neck, weakening him too quickly. He saw the wall to the next circle in the distance and decided to run for it. He galloped hard, his vision blurring with the increasing blood loss, and leapt over a group of humans who were pushing a giant boulder in their mad spell. Chiron's blood spilled onto the humans as he flew over them. The Master Centaur placed his hand flat against the wounded area of his neck to stem the flow. He was approaching the wall fast, and hoped the handholds to the Third Circle were more centaur-friendly.

When he reached the bottom of the wall, a slight slope provided a far easier climb. The rock had been chiseled and arranged to ease the ascent for bipeds, but it was good enough for four-leggeds. At the middle of the climb, Chiron lay out on an adjacent rock ledge, his hooves jutting over the Fourth Circle below him. He could see the feral Plutus far off, struggling to remove the arrow. Plutus's cries could be heard from even this great distance. Chiron, pushing his hand against his neck, felt the bleeding had slowed a little. He pulled out his last vial of water and drank deeply. The cool liquid was sweet and began its healing work immediately.

As he rested, observing the madness of the mobs below, he contemplated the future of Hell.

Chapter 44
Meeting the Father

Chiron kneeled his way across the windy landscape of the Second Circle. Above, tormented humans were cast about by the high winds. Violently and mercilessly twisted, they smashed against each other, and splattered against a far off cliff, the edge of which lead up to the First Circle. The winds were threatening his foothold and it was an unbearable trek. Centaurs have great difficulty kneeling for long periods of time. A few humans above, who were stopped momentarily as the wind shifted direction, had obviously never seen a centaur. If Chiron stood up on his hooves, he would have been swept up with the blustering crowd above.

Chiron grunted through the discomfort, continuing to hobble across the Second Circle. He could see the Hall of Minos ahead, just as Aristotle had described it. It was a large, stately building, once white and marbled, now dirty from many millennia of dust and wind. It stood small against the background of the rocky heights of the First Circle. By Chiron's standards, having been in the Seventh Circle for thousands of years, the Hall of Minos was huge.

The sight of the pillars took him back to his life in the ancient world, when the sun shone and night fell, and for a moment he could even remember the smell of the daylight. As he got closer to the building, Chiron apprehended a shadow, moving quickly toward him. He stopped moving, checking the wind to determine if it was powerful enough to sweep him away. The winds had been slowly diminishing as he neared the hall, but the shadow disappeared suddenly. Chiron waited, sniffing the air. Centaurs have a highly developed sense of smell, and on the occasion where there was danger, it was very helpful. Chiron strung his bow, and pointed it up, searching left and right, before the creature struck him from behind.

The beast ravaged his right shoulder, leaving several bleeding bite marks. Chiron dropped his bow. The beast had a hold on his upper right arm. Chiron reached with his left arm and tore the creature off, swinging the rabid beast around so he could confirm what he suspected. He pummeled it, unleashing his rage, as it squirmed and tried to bite him to escape his grip. It was a small, two headed imp, with tiny wings, and apparently must have flown quite fast to get behind him in the torrential winds. Only a severely unintelligent creature would try to attack a centaur, twenty times its size and as much stronger. They were vicious, stupid little insects to the centaurs, and the centaurs would not suffer their existence. This one would wander no more.

Chiron grabbed a hold of the small wings, holding one in each hand, and pulled. The beast shrieked loudly, though this was not enough to dispatch it. Taking the long knife out of his sack, Chiron thrust forward; the flailing imp became a shrieking puff of smoke, and was dissipated into the wind. Chiron replaced his weapon and rubbed his back, neck and arm where the imp had clawed into it. This wound was an irritation compared to that inflicted by Plutus, but caused Chiron to stop a few moments. The Master Centaur searched the air for more beasts as he checked his pack needlessly for a possible last vial. No water remained; Chiron would have to wait until he reached Limbo. He was almost there.

Chiron walked around the Hall of Minos and, noticing the long line of people, he trotted alongside, moving closer to the humans. The humans, believing they were in for the first of Hell's punishments, recoiled in fright. Chiron looked at them pityingly.

Far up the line stood a pair of imps. They had come around the other side of the Hall, and must have been in the same pack as the imp Chiron had just destroyed. The pair headed straight toward a horrified human. The closer they got, the more the man cowered. He tried to hide within the crowd, but everyone moved away from him as the beasts attacked. Chiron decided he would tolerate the beasts no longer.

He drew his bow. In a moment he would dispatch both creatures. But before the arrow was loosed, a thundering voice came from inside the great hall; a great booming voice that unnerved Chiron, and caused the humans to cry out in fear.

"Stinking hell spawn!" roared the voice. In a moment, Chiron could see its source. It was a large human, as tall as Chiron, muscular in build, and olive skinned. He walked proudly toward the cowering, savaged human. The imps were in a feeding frenzy and had not noticed the immense human bearing down upon them.

"Get off. These are not judged yet. Leave now or I will-" the voice stopped abruptly as the human saw Chiron. His surprise was great, so great that he stopped his motion toward the imperiled human.

"What is this?" he roared at Chiron. "Why are you here? Centaur-folk are not judged in this place." The human, whom Chiron assumed correctly to be Minos, stood in front of the Master Centaur, studying him.

"I am Chiron, of the centaurs of Phlegethon. I travel to Limbo with news for the citizenry therein."

Minos appeared puzzled. "And I am Minos, Judge of the Dead, Lord Chiron. This is my great Hall, where the dead come for assignment of their torment. How is it you travel freely through Hell, Master Centaur? Very few do so, and rarely are they not demon-kind. Never are they workers who have been assigned to any circle." Minos drew in closer and lowered his voice, "Have you learned to dispel the Fallen magic? You must have to have countered the spell that bound you to the Circle of Phlegethon."

"I have not used Fallen magic, King Minos. I have no training or ability with it. But it seems the spell which confined me and my kind to the Seventh Circle has been lifted, or diminished. I can provide no other explanation."

"What news have you to speak of to Limbo's untormented?" asked Minos, as he looked at the wounds on Chiron's back and neck.

"With respect, King Minos, that is private business."

Chiron was stern. A noise from behind the line reminded the two workers that the problem with the imps was still in progress. Chiron, in the blink of an eye, shot off an arrow into the neck of one of the creatures, which had climbed up onto the shoulder of the screaming man and was clawing the hair off of his head. The creature grabbed the arrow sticking out of both sides of its neck, unable to shriek, and then became a black cloud, as the arrow dropped through the smoke and onto the ground. Minos, in admiration, motioned to Chiron to let him take care of the remaining imp. As Chiron watched, the large human waved his arms, then spoke.

"I will show you something I have learned, Lord Chiron. *Bascaria – batah!*"

Chiron watched as the imp, terror on its face, went motionless, and then disappeared into a puff of black smoke as his companion had. It was effortless, and Chiron nodded his approval to Minos. The King smiled proudly. The attacked man sat on the path, still screaming, even with the beasts gone. Minos stared at him, and the small human stopped at once.

"That was Fallen magic. The hand waving was for my own dramatic emphasis," said Minos. Chiron smiled, and Minos turned back toward the hall. "Chiron, I would ask you to stay a while. I would like to speak with you, maybe even give you some knowledge to use on your trek. But I need to sit; the Fallen magic causes me to tire. Please, come into my hall. I have had no company for some time. Will you be returning to Phlegethon when you finish in Limbo?"

"Yes. I will return. I will come into your hall also."

"Very good. I must keep this line moving or the people will be backed up all the way to Acheron, and then I'll have to deal with Charon. He is so unsociable. We can speak while the crowd continues," said Minos.

"I believe I will enjoy a visit. This is the first time off my post in millennia," said Chiron. "I would also like to talk to you about your son." Minos turned quickly in surprise. He did not believe he had heard the Master Centaur correctly.

"I am sorry. I do not believe I heard you. Did you say my *son*?" asked Minos. "Do you know my son? Are you sure?"

"Asterion. I believe him to be your son. Am I incorrect?" asked Chiron.

"You are certain? My son is…" Minos paused, concerned as to whether he should continue.

He is Minotaur." said Chiron. "Half-human…like me."

Chapter 45
End of the Line

I stood in line for many days, or at least it seemed I did. The line moved slowly, and for awhile more people came up behind me and took their places in the back of the line. Curiously however, within a day's time, I noticed an end to the line coming from Acheron. That is, people stopped coming from the dock. The sobbing man was there but did not speak. He only leaned against the wall, grunting every so often, and breathing in short shallow gasps. I suspected he had broken ribs, but I was not going to ask him. He should have been faster getting away from Charon. I was still angry with him for that. Otherwise, like everyone else in line, I waited for eternal torment.

I thought this line must be the finale before meeting the judge of Hell. Minos was, according to Dante, the decider of the fate of all sinners. I was almost sure this was Dante's Hell, but I wasn't absolutely positive since there were no walls in Dante's Hell. Or at least, I did not remember the walls. I was sure there was only a path through Limbo before the line into the Hall of Minos. I guessed that Limbo must have been walled off to keep the sinners out, since there was, according to

Dante, no punishment there; certainly it would be a great place to wander into. I wondered how many people had 'accidentally' done that. But then again, no way would it be easy, right?

The line was about the worst I had ever been in. The worst, in life was at Disney World when I was nine years old, but that was because I was too young to wait. Here, I felt that impatience again. I did not want to move forward, but I didn't like waiting either. I looked at the sobbing man. He was standing better than before, having no trouble breathing. Perhaps Charon had not broken his ribs? Maybe he had some anxiety issues that caused him to breathe with difficulty? I looked behind him. The end of the line contained the same faces I had seen before. Was no one else dying?

I finally came to a place where I could see ahead. I saw a darker atmosphere in the far distance, and could hear the sound of high winds. Now I was certain where I was. A little while later I saw the destination of the line I spent so much time in. It led down into the Hall of Minos.

The Hall of Minos was a Parthenon type of architecture, with large columns. There was a thin path of steps rising slightly and leading into the structure. The building was lit up, though I saw no torches, light fixtures, or any other light sources. It was still in the distance, but I could see my path would soon become a crudely carved stairway. I glanced around, my eyes hungry for new scenery. I had seen only walls and miserable people for too long. I took in the new sights, searching for whatever lay ahead.

Down the path, toward the hall, there was some commotion. The people were making that noise a crowd makes when everyone becomes frightened or alarmed. Anticipating danger, I anxiously strained to see what had made them cry out. In a few moments, I saw a creature, coming out of the darkness, from the left side of the building. I squeezed my eyes shut, then slowly opened them.

Moving toward the line was a huge centaur. Where in Hell was I?

To be continued in

AngelFall
Book III

Available December 1st, 2011

Made in the USA
Lexington, KY
31 August 2012